Love's Bloom

SECOND CHANCE AT FIRST LOVE

ZOE ALLISON

SECOND CHANCE AT FIRST LOVE

Dedication

For the NHS workers of the UK and their counterparts throughout the world, who gave their everything during the 2020 pandemic.

Chapter One

Eva unloaded her bags from the car and surveyed the large house along the driveway. *Home sweet home.* Well, her parents' home anyway. It hadn't been hers in over a decade and now she'd come full circle. *Ugh, that's pretty depressing.*

She pulled on her shoulder bag, grasped the handle of her wheeled suitcase and lifted her tote. Trying not to trip on the uneven paving, she dragged her stuff to the front door. The scent of spring flowers caught her attention and she glanced over to where her mother's crocuses and hyacinths were blooming along the garden path. *Is it crocuses or croci?* Eva remembered the tale of a mischievous local man who'd been given community service for minor misdemeanours. His job had been to plant crocuses along the main road through their small Yorkshire town. After dutifully completing his task, he went on his way. That spring the blooms came into full force, planted in such a pattern as to spell out the most pearl-clutching of four-letter words. The women's bridge club had been most affronted, unlike the community teens, who gathered at every opportunity to take selfies by the flowery swear words before the local council cut them down.

Eva sniggered despite her low-key misery as she remembered the tale. She inhaled the sweet smell of her mother's hyacinths and reached for the doorbell, but before she could press it, the door whooshed open and she was enveloped in a hug. The scent of Chanel overpowered the flowers.

"Hi, Mum."

Her mother pulled back and studied her face. "Come in and get your feet up, *beti*, I'll make you a nice cup of tea."

Eva smiled at the sound of her pet name. It meant 'daughter' in her mum's native tongue, Urdu.

Her mother seemed to be under the impression that tea possessed healing powers that cured all ills. However, Eva wasn't sure it was strong enough for her current predicament. She climbed the stone steps into the house and set down her bags.

"Matthew!" her mum yelled. "Come get Eva's bags!"

Her dad appeared on the upstairs landing. "No need to shout, Meena. I'm right here."

Eva shook her head. "I can manage, Mum."

Matthew came down the stairs. "No, I'll get them." He enveloped her in another parental hug. Eva inhaled the soothing scent of his aftershave and was overcome by a flood of childhood memories.

She smiled against her father's chest. "For goodness sake, I'm being hugged to death here. Death by cuddle."

Matthew laughed and released her, grabbing her bags to take upstairs. Eva followed her mum along the hall into the kitchen and took a seat at the table.

Meena busied herself about the kitchen, brewing her signature tea to perfection. "How was your journey?"

Eva leaned back and gazed out of the patio doors onto her mum's well-kept back garden. "Fine. A bit of traffic going through Cumbria but, on the whole, not too bad."

Meena poured the tea into two china cups. "It's a bit of a boring journey on your own all the way from *Scot*land, isn't it?" Whenever Meena said 'Scotland' she attempted a terrible Scottish accent, which made Eva cringe and smile at the same time.

Meena brought the cups and saucers over and placed one in front of Eva. "I used to get fed up when I did the journey after dropping you off at university."

Eva sipped her tea. "I like listening to the radio. It takes my mind off things."

Meena nodded, shifting in her seat and fiddling with the milk jug. She cleared her throat. "When does the new job start?"

Eva grasped her cup, enjoying the warmth that transferred into her fingers. "I wanted to give myself enough time to get settled here, so I don't start until the beginning of next month."

Meena lit up. "Great. That gives us a few weeks to do some cool mother-daughter bonding."

Eva laughed. The word 'cool' wasn't her mum's usual vernacular. "Sounds awesome."

She sipped at her tea again. Meena Mathers did indeed make a mean brew and it was soothing—but unfortunately not problem-solving. Eva doubted there was any solution to her problems. She shook her head in an attempt to dispel those thoughts and shifted her gaze from the floral pattern on the cup over to her mother. "What room am I in?"

Meena placed her teacup down with a clatter. "Your old room, of course. Go and have a nosy. I've redecorated for you coming."

Eva raised her eyebrows. "Aw, Mum, you didn't need to do that."

"I wanted to," Meena said, reaching over and topping up their cups. "I thought it would be nice for it to look different from when…" She trailed off, her cheeks flushing.

Eva smiled. "What? From when I was last here with Callum?"

Meena glanced up from where she'd been stirring her tea a little too aggressively. "Well…yes. Sorry. My mouth ran away with me. I need to engage the brain before speaking, as you keep telling me."

Eva stood and hugged her. "It's okay. You're allowed to mention him. I'll go have a peek at the room."

Meena smiled and kissed her cheek.

Eva left the kitchen and climbed the stairs, walking along the hallway to her old bedroom. Sunlight enveloped the space in a bright haze. It really did appear different. Interior design was Meena's passion, along with gardening and tea drinking. So, as a British-Pakistani, she fitted right into the Yorkshire tea culture.

None of those things were Eva's interests but she could appreciate that the room looked good. She ran her hand across the bedspread, trying not to think about the fact that last time she was here at Christmas, Callum had shared the bed with her.

She made her way around the room, unpacking and putting clothing and other items into drawers and the wardrobe. She found the paperwork for her new job at the Riverside Medical Practice, which was in the neighbouring town, and placed it neatly into her doctor's bag. She thought of her friends and colleagues at her old practice in Edinburgh and how supportive they'd been when she'd handed in her notice. '*We're so sorry to see you go,*' the senior partner had said, '*but everyone understands your need to return home for support after all that's happened.*'

The requirement for family support wasn't the only reason for her leaving. There was also the need to put as much distance between her and Callum as possible, plus to give herself mental space from her pain. She'd become adept at burying it. If she didn't think about it, then she was over it. *Right?*

Eva wandered back down the stairs and into the living room. She plonked onto the sofa next to her dad.

Matthew glanced away from the horse racing on TV, raising his eyebrow. "Still bouncing me off the sofa whenever you sit down, I see."

Eva grinned. "Shut up, Dad."

Meena entered the room carrying a tray containing yet more tea. She cleared her throat loudly as she placed it on the coffee table. "Matthew, that was Lily on the phone. She says Damon and Sarah are *definitely* splitting up."

Eva was only half listening as she studied the messages on her cell phone. Her friends back in Scotland were texting to ask if she'd gotten there safely, and her best friend here in Oakcastle had contacted her to suggest meeting up. She glanced at Meena. *Funny, I didn't hear the landline ring.* Her mum's best friend Lily always called the house phone rather than Meena's mobile.

Matthew raised his eyebrows. "Oh yes? She *just* called, did she?"

Eva gave them her full attention. Her dad used that tone when mum was up to something.

Meena nodded. "She was on the phone a moment ago." She sat in an armchair and gazed at the ceiling. "It's *such* a shame, isn't it?" She let out a loud sigh. "We were hoping they'd manage to work out their problems for the sake of the children. But Sarah said it had to end, that they seemed more like brother and sister than a couple. Poor Damon is heartbroken."

"Damon?" said Eva, finally realizing who they were talking about. Her mum's best friend's son was someone she hadn't thought about in a while. They'd been in the same year at school and Damon had been Eva's first love. Though it was a shame that she hadn't been his—and that he hadn't noticed her at all.

"Wow, that's so sad," said Eva, "especially when they have two kids. And they've been together forever." Damon and Sarah had been going out since before she and Callum had met. They'd never married but were so solid in their relationship and had gone on to have a daughter named Adele and a son called Sam. Eva pursed her lips and blew out a deep breath. *Everyone is splitting up nowadays. Has it come to that time of life already? I'm not even thirty yet.*

Eva glanced at her dad. He had a wry expression on his face. She rolled her eyes. Auntie Lily hadn't just phoned. They'd clearly discussed this piece of bad news a while before, and here Mum was trying to mention it in a nonchalant way for Eva's benefit...and failing badly.

In the past, Meena Mathers and Lily Evans would've loved nothing more than for their two offspring to become a couple, though neither of them had known about Eva's feelings for Damon during their school days together. No one did, because she'd never confided in anyone. She wasn't comfortable voicing those kinds of emotions for fear of appearing foolish, especially when it was regarding a ridiculous crush on someone who was way out of her league.

Eva preferred to play her cards close to her chest. The more she liked someone, the more inclined she was to keep it quiet. The only reason she and Callum had gotten together was because he'd made the first move — and the second, third and fourth... He was super-confident and always went after what he wanted. Sometimes Eva wished she were more like him.

Eva played dumb to her mother's game and acted like she wasn't interested, even though old feelings were starting to surface. She remembered Damon's warm brown eyes and his playful smile. They'd only had one class together in high school and she'd deliberately chosen the seat behind him so that she could stare at the back of his head. He had dark brown hair with a soft curl and she used to fantasize about running her hands through it.

Eva shook her head. *Stop being an idiot. That was a lifetime ago.* "I suppose that was the saving grace for Callum and me. No kids. So I don't ever have to see the bastard again."

Normally she'd expect a 'Language, Eva,' from her mother. But on this occasion, Meena must've thought it well deserved because not only did she let the comment pass but it appeared she was nodding in agreement.

Matthew stared at the TV. "Good riddance to bad rubbish."

Eva glanced over. He was normally good at hiding it, but since their split, she'd gotten the feeling he'd never really liked Callum.

"So," Meena said, "Damon has moved out into a lovely house a bit down the road from Auntie Lily, and Sarah and the kids are staying in the family home.

Damon gets them every other weekend. You should see his house, Eva. It is *huge*. His company is doing really well."

Eva raised her eyebrows. "Wow. That house sale was organised very quickly when Auntie Lily's *just* called you to tell you they only *just* split up."

Matthew snorted with stifled laughter.

"Yes, I know," Meena said, her cheeks colouring. "Anyway, I'm just going to check on dinner."

Meena left the room and Eva and her dad both broke down laughing.

Eva shook her head. "She's hilarious. She never changes."

Matthew smiled. "I know—and I wouldn't want her to."

Eva cuddled into his side. Her mum and dad were the best, and she was lucky to have such loving parents who cared for her, her big sister and each other in equal measure. "Dad?"

"Yes?"

"Can I ask you something?"

"Is it about Callum?"

Her dad had always been exceptional at reading her. He was the most intuitive man she knew. "Yes."

He sighed. "Before you ask... No, I never liked him. He wasn't right for you or good enough for you either."

Matthew Mathers was also very matter of fact when his opinion was requested.

Eva met his gaze. "What makes you say that?"

Matthew frowned. "He didn't appreciate you. Treated you like some sort of trophy and didn't look out for you."

She grimaced. "I don't need looking after. I'm a grown woman and my actual job is to take care of other people."

He smiled. "I know, and you're very good at it. But what I mean is the way a husband and wife *both* look out for each other and put one another first."

Put one another first. Callum had never put her first, always himself. He was out for number one and did what he wanted without any regard for her needs or feelings. Looking back, she wondered how she hadn't noticed the warning signs earlier, but they'd been madly in love. Then, as time had gone on, she had just accepted how he operated, though she'd never dreamed in her worst nightmares how things would end. *I was a supreme idiot for falling for his crap, so maybe I deserved everything I got.*

* * * *

Damon kicked off his shoes and followed the smell of steak pie into his mother's kitchen. Lily stood in front of the stove, dabbing at her eyes with a tissue.

He went over and hugged her. "You okay? Your eyes are red."

Lily cleared her throat and smiled. "I was just chopping onions."

Damon studied the kitchen counter. "There're no onions here."

Lily waved her hand and opened the oven to check on the pie. "That's because I've started cooking them already, silly."

He touched her arm. "Mum."

She shut the oven door. "I'm fine, honestly."

Footsteps sounded on the hallway flooring and Alastair Evans came through the kitchen door. He grinned and strode towards Damon to ruffle his hair. "Alright champ, how you doing?"

Damon ducked his head. "Watch it, old man. This do is styled to perfection."

"Yeah, right." Alastair laughed. "Dragged through a hedge backward more like."

Damon smiled. His dad's answer was to be jovial and make a joke out of every situation. Light relief was welcome in Damon's book, especially right now. But he could tell his mum was lying about the onions, and he knew what she'd really been crying about.

Damon helped dish up and the three of them sat down to dinner. Lily chattered away about all the latest gossip and Alastair interjected with rubbish cheesy jokes. Damon watched them, smiling. He was glad they were all laughing together, because he was guilty that his situation upset his mum so much. Lily still had Adele and Sam once a week when he and Sarah were working, plus she saw them on his weekends. Her contact with her grandchildren hadn't diminished, but she was devastated that his family had fractured and that he was so torn up by it.

Damon wasn't particularly upset about splitting with Sarah. Their relationship had been over for a while, but he'd just put a brave face on it for everyone. It was the fact that he was no longer living full time with his kids that got to him. Only seeing them every other weekend was alien.

At least he was a master of his own destiny when it came to his career. Being a partner in his own company meant he could work flexibly from home and see more of Adele and Sam in the week. He and Sarah were still fine-tuning the details. Their relationship was amicable, which made shared parenting so much easier.

He studied his mum while she gossiped to his dad. Maybe he should take her to one side and reassure her that everything was going to be okay. He'd tried already, but she couldn't stop worrying and trying to find little distractions for him. He tuned back in to the conversation between his parents.

Lily waved her hand in the air. "...so that's Eva just arrived home this afternoon."

"Mm-hmm," replied Alastair, looking at the TV over Lily's shoulder.

Lily turned to Damon. "It's a shame, isn't it?"

He paused, his fork en route to his mouth. "What's a shame?"

Lily sighed. "About poor Eva and that nasty Callum."

Damon frowned. "Eva Mathers? What about her and Callum?"

Damon hadn't seen much of Eva since she'd gone to university. She'd married a Scottish guy called Callum but he'd only met him once, at Eva's sister's wedding. He and Sarah had been invited to Eva and Callum's wedding, along with the rest of his family, but in the end, only Lily and Alastair had gone because Sarah had been heavily pregnant with Adele at the time.

Lily raised her eyebrows. "Remember I told you a few months ago they'd split up? And Eva decided to leave her job in Edinburgh and come home to stay with her parents. Well, she's back now and she'll be starting a new job nearby."

Damon shook his head. "You didn't tell me that. I would've remembered."

Lily's set her mouth in a hard line. "I doubt it. You've been so distracted by the kerfuffle between you and Sarah that you hardly listen to a word I say anymore...like your father. Though he never listens to me anyway," she added under her breath.

"What's that, dear?" Alastair replied, right on cue.

Lily rolled her eyes.

Damon took a sip of his drink. "What happened between them?"

Lily shook her head. "I don't know. Meena does, but she's sworn to silence. She's the only one Eva's told, except Matthew, of course. But it must be really bad, because Meena called Callum the 'C' word."

Damon nearly choked on his dinner. "She called him *what*?"

"You know," whispered Lily. "*Crap*."

"Phew," said Damon, glancing at Alastair, who was doubled up with laughter.

"It's not funny," Lily said. "The poor girl's devastated. She's had to give up the GP partnership she worked so hard for to get away from it all."

Damon leaned back in his seat. *Eva Mathers*. They'd played together as kids. Not only were their mothers best friends but their older sisters had also been as well. The two of them were in each other's company a lot and had become good friends. But they'd drifted apart through high school because they'd ended up mixing with different crowds. She was very academic and worked hard. He'd always known she'd go off to university and become a doctor or a lawyer or something. For him, school had been a laugh. He wasn't bothered about studying, just chased girls and had fun. In Eva he remembered a feisty girl at primary who had morphed into a shy, quiet one at high school. It had likely been a defence mechanism because being smart hadn't made you very popular at their school. When they had been younger, she'd given him a run for his money—always an answer for his cheeky comments. Later in their school careers, if their paths ever crossed, he'd just gotten a 'Get lost, Damon', and she'd walk off.

Lily was staring at him. "What's your opinion on it?"

He focused his attention back on his mum. "On what?"

Lily huffed out her breath. "On Eva and Callum, of course." She shook her head. "I don't know why I even bother talking to you pair."

Damon smiled. "I hardly think my opinion matters. I'm not much of a relationship expert, am I?"

"Well," said Lily, "I just wondered, seeing as you two are in the same boat..."

Damon laughed. "Yeah. I'll need to get her number to call to see if she wants to start an Oakcastle lonely hearts club."

"Good idea," Lily said.

Damon paused. "I was being sarcastic, Mum."

Lily's face fell. "Oh right. Well, I'll just get the pudding sorted." She stood and went over to the kitchen counter.

Normally Damon would offer to help, but he was too distracted. For some reason, Eva had settled into his brain. She'd always been really pretty but lacking in confidence. He couldn't remember her having a boyfriend at school. The first one he'd known about was when they were eighteen at sixth form college, although he hadn't seen as much of her then because he'd dropped out to start his own business. In contrast to Eva, Damon had had a different girlfriend every month at school.

He wondered how many others from their year were now coming out of long-term relationships. *God, I feel old.*

Damon was talked into staying over at his parents and having brunch with them the next morning. He didn't have anything to do until the following afternoon and being home alone in that big house just made him miss the kids more acutely, so he agreed.

As he settled into bed in his old room, he found Eva drifting across his thoughts again. It was funny how someone he hadn't seen in years could start playing on his mind constantly. He drifted off to sleep, dreaming that he was back in school, turning round in his chair and seeing Eva's dark curly hair flicking as she turned her head towards the window. He'd always gotten the feeling that she'd been looking at him seconds before. But that couldn't be right, could it? She'd definitely thought he was a bit of an idiot.

Chapter Two

The next morning Eva had been sent to the small shop along the road from her parents' to get some eggs for breakfast. The day was bright and cloudless, so she'd decided to walk.

She arrived and started wandering up and down the narrow aisles. It was a new place and unfamiliar to her. She couldn't for the life of her spot where the eggs were. Then she rounded a corner and walked smack bang into someone.

"Oops, sorry." She glanced up at the man she'd collided with, heat rising in her cheeks.

Damon smiled. "That's okay. I got pretty used to being knocked about by you at school."

Eva stood open-mouthed for a second before she remembered herself. "Sorry… I wasn't looking where I was going."

He grinned. "That's okay. I think you've broken my foot, though. Good job you're a doctor. You can fix it for me."

Eva laughed, trying to cover the fact that a million butterflies had suddenly nested in her stomach. "No problem. As long as your feet don't smell." *Oh my God, what's wrong with me? Why did I just say that?*

Damon raised an eyebrow, and Eva's knees were suddenly the consistency of jelly.

"How dare you," he said. "I'll have you know every part of me smells great."

Eva watched him for a second, trying really hard not to think about the fact that he still was great-looking, never mind smelling — or the fact that her flirting game was well below par. Who else would tell their biggest lifetime crush that their feet smelled?

To her relief, a smile played at the corners of his mouth, indicating that he'd taken her stupid comment in good humour. Perhaps she'd manage the rest of the conversation without alienating him after all.

Damon met her gaze. "You're back in town then. Mum says you've got a new job in Silverbridge?"

Eva swallowed in an attempt to lubricate her dry mouth. "Yeah, that's right. I missed the place so much I decided to come home, you know? It's party central down here."

Damon laughed. "What were you searching for when you decided to rugby-tackle me?"

Eva scanned the shelves. "Eggs. Mum forgot them for breakfast."

Damon frowned. "Hmm. Same here. Our mothers are still very alike."

Eva raised her eyebrows. *That sounds suspicious. They both needed the exact same thing from the local shop at the same precise moment?*

Damon led her to the end of the aisle where the eggs were stacked and grabbed a couple of boxes. "Allow me, Madam."

"Why thank you," Eva said. "You really know how to spoil a girl." Damon did a mock bow and went to the counter to pay.

They headed out onto the street together, Damon sporting a plastic, egg-containing bag on his wrist.

"So," Eva said, thinking carefully in order not to come out with any more ridiculous statements. "What's the hometown gossip?"

Damon rubbed his chin. "Let me think. The big news stories are...woman seen hanging out washing, man drinks pint in pub and...milkman delivers milk ten minutes late."

Eva blew out a big breath. "Wow. That exciting, huh?"

He glanced over, smiling. "Yup. Can hardly contain it. This place is a pumping hive of sin."

Eva tried to stop images associated with sin and Damon crowding her thoughts. She cleared her throat. "Do you see anyone from school?"

He nodded. "I'm still friends with a few of the guys. John and Steve are both married with kids and Dave is currently single. Those of us who're fathers are considered to be late starters, though. There're a couple of blokes from our year who've got about six kids with various women."

Eva's eyes widened. "What?"

"Yep." He ran his hand across the air in front of him, as if tracing a newspaper headline. "Haven't you heard about Eric Donovan, serial father?"

She shook her head. "Sounds like something off a terrible talk show. I remember Eric but I didn't know he had loads of kids. Come to think of it, I'm struggling to think how he got one woman to shag him, never mind several."

Damon laughed. "I know what you mean. I don't understand how the guy has any game. Remember when he pretended that he'd been in a porn film?"

Eva covered her face with her hand. "Oh my God, I forgot about that. He thought it would impress the girls, but it just made everybody feel nauseated"

He smiled. "What did he say the name of it was again?"

Eva shook her head. "Eric does Oakcastle."

Damon laughed so hard that he had to pause for a second and hold his stomach. "That was it! Bloody hell that was a classic."

Eva smiled. "The film...or his story?"

He grinned. "His story. There's still no evidence of the film's actual existence. Trust me... I've done the research."

Eva's butterflies were rapidly evaporating. She still suffered a surge in heart rate when she looked at him, but it was so easy to be in his presence, even after all this time. They reached the crossroads where Damon needed to turn left to get his parents'. It was just a few houses down the street. They came to a standstill.

Eva turned to him. "So is your new house nearby?"

He nodded, pointing over the crest of the next hill. "See that chimney there? That's mine."

Eva peered into the distance. "One of the new builds? They're lovely."

"Thanks," he said. "I'm settling in, gradually."

She smiled. "Well it was good to bump into you...literally."

He grinned. "Thanks, I enjoyed it too. Next time I've got a few ribs you can break."

She laughed. "Come on. I hardly touched you." She nudged his arm gently.

Damon grabbed his arm in mock pain and stuck out his bottom lip. "Ow."

Eva made a show of rolling her eyes, though secretly her insides were churning just at the touch of his jacketed arm. She didn't want their encounter to be over. She smiled. "Hopefully I'll see you around."

Damon nodded. "I'm sure our paths will cross. See ya."

Eva turned to head for home, then he shouted her name and she paused, her pulse picking up. *Maybe he's going to ask for my number?*

Damon came back towards her. "You forgot the eggs. Meena will disown you if you come back empty-handed."

Eva's heart sank. *Of course.* Damon handed her the box. Their fingers brushed as she took it from him, sending a million volts of electricity shooting up her arm, and she only just avoided the container slipping from her grasp. She caught Damon's gaze and for a split second their eyes locked. Had he felt that too? No he probably thought she was an idiot for nearly dropping the box.

She cleared her throat. "Thank you."

He glanced into the middle distance for a second, then ran a hand through his hair. "No problem. Okay, well. See ya... Wouldn't wanna be ya."

She smiled. That was one of their old sayings from when they had been kids. She waved as she turned to go. It took all her willpower not to sneak a look back over her shoulder at him. She started walking but it was a couple of minutes until her heart rate normalized. He was even more handsome than she remembered and really fit too. Even with that brief touch to his arm over his jacket, she'd been able to feel solid biceps underneath. *What's wrong with me? I'm not sixteen anymore.*

On arriving home, Meena greeted her right as she got through the door. "Oh great, *beti*. You got the eggs."

Eva raised her eyebrows. "Why wouldn't I have gotten them? They're not exactly a rarity."

"Oh, no reason, no reason," Meena said, taking the box from her. "See anyone you knew?"

Eva stifled a laugh. That was confirmation that her mum and Auntie Lily had engineered the scenario. She decided to torture Meena. "No," she said, "I didn't see anyone. Why?"

Meena hesitated. "Oh, I'm just interested, that's all. Anyway, I'll get our brunch going." She turned and disappeared into the kitchen.

Eva cursed under her breath. *You're onto a losing game there, Mum.*

Chapter Three

Eva awoke the next morning with palpitations. In her dream she'd been back in the corner shop standing in a deserted aisle when Damon strode up, grasped her around the waist with one arm and behind the head with the other, then brought his lips down onto hers and kissed her passionately. He was pushing her up against the shelf of tinned goods in order to ravish her when she came to. She sighed, aggrieved that she'd woken up at the good bit. It dawned on her that it was the first night since the whole Callum debacle that she hadn't dreamt about her ex-husband, so that was plus, though a pity that the latest dream was unobtainable.

She padded downstairs in her dressing gown and slippers and took a seat at the kitchen table. Her mum was busying around the kitchen and paused to set a steaming cup of tea in front of her. Eva smiled. *If I stay here much longer, I'm going to die of a tea overdose.*

Meena glanced over. "What're you smiling at?"

Eva shook her head. "Nothing. What's the plan for today's mother-daughter bonding extravaganza?"

Meena sat next to her, rubbing her hands together. "I've got a couple of things planned. You're going to love it."

Eva raised her eyebrows. So far her mum's sneaky activities hadn't been to her taste. "What sort of things?"

Meena smiled. "I've got us a treatment booked at the new spa at Alton Hall, then lunch in the main hotel. After that, a little shopping trip so I can treat you to some nice new clothes."

Eva smiled with relief. "That's sounds great. But you really don't need to buy me anything. I can get my own clothes."

Meena shrugged. "I want to. You need a nice wardrobe to start your new job." She lifted her wrist to check her watch. "We should probably get ready because the treatments are at ten a.m."

Eva nodded and finished the last of her tea. "Okay. I'll just grab a shower."

The drive to Alton Hall was beautiful through the Yorkshire countryside. As Eva gazed onto the sun-tinted fields, she let her mind drift and relax, starting to feel more confident that a move back here could help her on the road to recovery from her messy marriage breakup and the trauma she'd been through. Memories from her previous job started to surface and she expertly shoved them to the back of her mind, something she was well practiced at.

They turned along the sweeping driveway, which led to the stately home that'd been turned into an upmarket hotel over two decades earlier. The spa was a new addition that Eva had yet to see.

Meena checked them into the spa reception and they were led through to a sunlit sitting room with wicker chairs to await their therapists. Ambient music was playing in the background.

Eva leaned back. "Ah, this is the life." She glanced at Meena, who was sipping at a cup of peppermint tea. *Does this woman ever miss an opportunity to drink tea?*

A therapist entered the room to call Meena. As she disappeared through the door, another spa employee entered to call Eva.

The pretty blonde therapist smiled. "Eva Mathers, is that you?"

It was someone Eva recognised. "Jane! Long time, no see."

Jane indicated for Eva to follow her through the door and they started along a low-lit hallway. "I know. I don't think I've seen you since school. What a nice surprise. Are you home for the weekend?"

Eva hesitated. "No…I'm back for a while."

Jane opened a door and gestured for Eva to enter. "Let's have a chat while I do your manicure."

The treatment room was warm and welcoming, and a soothing scent lingered in the air. Eva sat at the manicure table and Jane took out some oils and started massaging her hands. *Maybe if I just stay here forever? I can relax and never think about Callum again…* She shook her head in order to knock his name out of it. She smiled at Jane. "How long have you worked here?"

"Ever since it opened," Jane said, placing Eva's hands into a warm soak. "It's such a great place."

Eva watched her take out various bottles and equipment, remembering how Jane's easy optimism had always been an attractive feature at school, despite them not being close friends.

Jane dried off Eva's hands. "How're things going for you, career-wise? I think it was medicine you went into?"

Eva nodded. "I work in general practice."

Jane took out a bottle and started painting Eva's nails. "Still in Scotland?"

Eva hesitated. "Up until now, yes." She cleared her throat. "Do you see anyone from school?"

Jane deftly moved from one nail to the next with her brush. "A couple of people. You tend to hear a lot of the gossip from just a few mouths." She glanced up to meet Eva's eyes and smiled, before returning her gaze to the task in hand. "Speaking of which," Jane added. "Did you hear the bad news about Damon and Sarah?"

The sound of his name caused an image of his smile to flash through her mind. "Yes, I did. It's a shame it didn't work out."

Jane set her mouth in a thin line. "Not for some people. Tracey seemed quite pleased to hear about it."

Eva frowned. "Tracey McKenna?"

Jane nodded.

Tracey was a fellow pupil in their year at school. She hadn't been Eva's favourite person because she used to bitch about all the girls, especially Eva, behind their backs.

Tracey had, however, been very popular as far as the boys had been concerned and had totted up many a notch on her bedpost during her teenage years. Rumour had it that she'd been Damon's first. That'd been a bitter pill for Eva to swallow at the time.

Eva blinked. "Isn't that water under the bridge?"

"You'd have thought so," Jane said. "We aren't sixteen anymore. But Tracey is a friend of a friend and apparently she still carries a torch for him. She's been single for a while since she broke up with her long-term partner."

Eva sighed. "Everyone's splitting up at the moment. It's thoroughly depressing."

Jane glanced at Eva's face. "Are you okay?"

Eva swallowed. "I suppose the rumour mill will turn to me before too long, so I might as well come clean. My husband and I are getting divorced."

Jane frowned. "I'm sorry. Here's me blabbing about relationships ending and making you feel bad."

Eva shook her head. "No need to apologize. I need to get over it sooner or later. It's been nearly five months."

"Has it?" Jane said. "Are you going to stay here permanently?"

Eva nodded. "There's nothing keeping me in Scotland now. I'd always intended to come back here so I could be near my family, and Callum was the only thing stopping me."

Jane returned to nail painting. "Are you staying with your parents?"

Eva watched Jane stroke the varnish down her nail. "Yeah, for now…until I figure out what I want."

Jane glanced up. "If you need anything, just ask. Perhaps we can get a drink sometime. Do you still see Rachel? Maybe the three of us could meet up."

Eva nodded. "Rachel and I are still close. We're going to get together one night soon. I can let you know when. It'd be fab if you could join us."

"Great." Jane smiled. "I'll slip a card with my number into your bag. I don't want you smudging your nails."

After they'd finished, Eva met up with Meena and they had lunch in the hotel restaurant.

Eva leaned back in her chair, rubbing her full belly. "I could get used to this." She grinned. "Are you going to treat me every weekend now that I'm home?"

Meena set her teacup down. "Ha. I'm not made of money. But it'd be lovely to make time for us to get together, especially once you get your own place." Meena took Eva's hand. "Though you know I'd love to have you stay forever."

Eva gave her mother's hand a squeeze. "Thank you. So, where to now?"

"Let's head to the shops and get you some nice things."

Two work outfits, two sparkly tops and one little black dress later, they loaded their purchases into Meena's car.

Eva closed the boot. "Thanks, Mum. I never would've thought to try on that dress. On the hanger it looked like it wouldn't suit me."

Meena raised her eyebrows. "It's always best to try things, Eva, otherwise you'll never know."

Meena had persuaded Eva to wear one of her new tops home. It was loose with a scoop neck and gathered at the waist, accentuating her curves.

Meena checked her watch before they got into the car.

Eva frowned. "Are you worried we'll be late home for Dad?"

Meena cleared her throat. "No. It's just I said I would pop into Lily's on the way back. I need to drop something off that I borrowed."

Eva settled into her seat. "No worries. It'd be nice to see Auntie Lily."

Meena smiled. "Great."

Chapter Four

They pulled up outside Lily and Alastair's house. Meena turned to Eva. "Go ring the doorbell, *beti*. I just need to get something out of the boot."

Eva unbuckled and climbed out while her mum went to the rear of the vehicle. She walked over to the front door and a small movement caught the corner of her eye. She could've sworn that the living room curtain had just twitched. She stared for a moment but couldn't see anyone. *Must've been my imagination.*

She pressed the doorbell and waited. There was a delay and she looked over her shoulder to see what was taking Meena so long. She was rummaging around in the boot. The sound of the door opening caused Eva to turn her head back and she smiled, ready to greet Lily. However the person answering the door was tall and handsome rather than small and feminine.

"Damon," she said, her mouth drying up. For a moment she couldn't think what to say. "Sorry… We weren't expecting to see you. Mum just needed to drop something off for Auntie Lily."

He did a double take, glancing down at her new top and back to meet her gaze. "No worries. It's great to see you both." He smiled. "Come in. Mum was here but she had to rush off to the bathroom just as you rang the bell."

The twitch of the curtain entered Eva's mind but it was swept away as she passed Damon and her arm skimmed his. A thousand goosebumps erupted out of nowhere.

Meena followed her, giving Damon a quick peck on the cheek. Eva wished she'd thought of doing that. She eyed her mother who, despite her rummaging in the car, had no such 'borrowed' item on her person.

Damon took them along the hallway into the kitchen. "Mum," he said, frowning. "I thought you were upstairs?"

"No," Lily said. "I mean, yes, I was. But I'm back down now." She hugged Meena and Eva.

Meena touched Damon's arm. "It's so nice to see you. We weren't expecting it."

Damon's frown gave way to a smile. "You too, Auntie Meena. You're looking fantastic, as always."

Eva smiled. Damon always had that easy way with people. He was charming and flirtatious. When she'd been younger, she'd constantly analyse the compliments he gave her, desperate to read more into them but knowing it was just his nature — and he was the same with everyone.

She gazed on while he spoke to her mum, admiring his smile and the curve of his lips. His hair was different today, styled a little higher over his head and brushed back, even more tempting for running her fingers through. He was wearing a white T-shirt that showed off his natural tan and honed biceps. She thought about the brush of his arm against hers when she'd entered the house and she shivered.

Lily squeezed Eva's shoulders. "I was thinking Damon should do the gentlemanly thing and take Eva out one evening for a drink. He can update her on all the young people's things going on in Oakcastle nowadays."

Eva glanced from Damon's physique to his face. He raised his eyebrow at his mother. Then he locked eyes with Eva and the butterflies that were already gathering in her stomach went into overdrive. He held her gaze for a moment then glanced back at the two older women. "I think you should let Eva decide who she wants to hang out with."

Lily and Meena looked at Eva. She cleared her throat. "I don't want to put Damon out. I'm sure he's got better things to do than babysit me."

"Nonsense," Lily said. "What's your number? Damon, get out your phone and put it in. Then he can face-chat you, or whatever it's called, to arrange something."

Damon shrugged and obeyed. Eva momentarily forgot her own number then managed to stutter out the digits. He typed them into his phone. As he lifted his T-shirt to place the phone back in his pocket, Eva caught a glimpse of toned abdomen and nearly fainted on the spot.

Lily and Meena finished their conversation with Eva feeling awkward on the outskirts. Then Meena declared they needed to get back because Matthew was making them dinner.

Lily led them to the door with Damon bringing up the rear behind Eva. Eva watched the two mums hug goodbye as if they weren't going to meet again for months, even though they were getting together the next day for badminton.

Damon leaned to whisper in her ear. The sensation of his breath on her cheek sent a shiver down her spine and her heart into overdrive. "I'll send you a text, or maybe 'face-chat' you later."

She turned to him and he was grinning at his mother's expense. He gave her a wink, turning her legs to jelly.

She managed a smile then gave a conspiratorial tap of her finger to the side of her nose. Damon laughed.

After they'd left the house, Eva again found herself analysing his behaviour, searching for any clues that he might feel even an iota of the attraction that she had towards him but there was nothing. He'd sounded reluctant to get her number then was nonchalant when he took it, even making a joke out of the whole thing at the end. She needed to get over it and accept that he only saw her as a friend.

Damon went back into his house, through the living room and collapsed onto the sofa. His trip to the gym hadn't had the desired effect. He still couldn't stop thinking about Eva.

He sighed. She may have been really pretty at school but nowadays she was downright drop-dead gorgeous. Her shoulder-length hair was wavy and dark with flecks of red, and it framed her green eyes. Her figure hadn't escaped his notice either. She'd been dressed casually at the shop the previous morning, but her curves had still been apparent under her fitted hoodie and skinny jeans.

After he'd called her back to give her the eggs, he'd nearly asked her for her phone number but decided that'd be inappropriate. The woman had only just arrived home after the heartbreak of her marriage ending. She didn't need some guy she hardly knew anymore sleazing on her.

When his mum had mysteriously asked him to pop over and change a light bulb, he hadn't been expecting to see Eva but was delighted that he had, albeit taken off guard. It appeared as though she were dressed to go out somewhere in that sparkly top that accentuated her gorgeous curves. He ran a hand through his hair. Was she going out later on? *Is she seeing someone?* The idea of that made him feel sick for some reason. *Surely she hasn't been home long enough to meet anyone yet?* But then again someone like her must get loads of attention. She was beautiful, intelligent and witty to boot.

He groaned and lifted his phone. Ever since the chance meeting earlier that day, he'd repeatedly gone to text her then chickened out and put the phone away again. He didn't know what to do. He wanted to message her but he kept remembering the expression of horror on her face when his mum had suggested he get her number, and the fact that she'd tried to get out of it by saying she didn't want him to babysit her.

He stared at the phone screen. But he *did* say he'd text, and he really would like to see her again, even if she only wanted to be friends. Finally he decided to bite the bullet.

So, Dr. Mathers, if I didn't know better, I'd say our mums are trying to set us up.

He put the phone down and tried to forget about it but ended up checking it every minute until it buzzed with Eva's reply.

What? Really? No way

Yes, really. My brilliant powers of deduction have concluded this.

Nice one, Sherlock. You really are a genius.

Ha! You're right. I am. Seriously though, if you do want a grab a drink sometime – just as friends of course – that'd be cool. Would be good to catch up.

That sounds great. Whenever you're free is fine by me. My social calendar is a bit light right now.

Damon sighed. She'd hooked on the idea after he'd said it'd be just as friends. He figured adding that part would be the only way she'd go for it. But that was fine. He was happy to be friends, if nothing else.

I've got the kids this weekend, but how about the weekend after? I'll treat you to a drink in the Swan next Saturday night. Please try to contain your excitement.

Brilliant. Looking forward to seeing whether my feet still stick to the carpet. Will text you nearer then to arrange time.

He smiled as he put his phone away. Maybe nothing romantic would ever happen between them, but he could never have too many friends.

Chapter Five

Eva brushed her hair then applied a little makeup. She was excited to see Rachel and Jane and have a proper talk. It'd been months since she'd seen Rachel face to face. They'd been best friends since school.

She smoothed down the sparkly top that she'd last worn on the afternoon Meena and Lily had ambushed her and Damon. She remembered Damon's texts from that night and her heart lifted at the thought of seeing him again but then sank a little on thinking how he'd deliberately spelt out the 'just as friends' part. She shook her head. It'd still be great to see him. They got on well and she needed all the friends she could get right now. Matthew gave Eva a lift into town. On pulling up outside the bar, he looked at her. "Be careful that there aren't any scoundrels in there trying to get their hands on you."

Eva laughed. "Don't worry, Dad. I've had enough of scoundrels to last a lifetime."

Matthew glanced at her with a smile. "Good."

She kissed his cheek and left the vehicle to head for the entrance. On passing through the doorway, she scanned the room for her friends. They were waving from a table by the window.

Eva approached and Rachel jumped up to grab her in a tight hug. "Missed you."

"Missed you too," Eva said. "But I can't breathe. You're bloody strong."

Rachel released her and grinned, her dark poker-straight bob framing her smile.

Eva sat next to Jane and gave her a hug too. She turned back to Rachel. "How're Marcus and the girls?"

Rachel smiled. "Who cares? I'm out for the evening."

Eva laughed. "What're you guys drinking?"

"Champagne cocktails," Rachel said. "We're celebrating."

Eva frowned. "Celebrating what?"

Rachel took a sip of her drink. "You being back home — and also being rid of Callum the arsehole."

Jane coughed on her drink and glanced at Eva.

Eva smiled. "You know what? That sounds like a great idea." She signalled a passing waiter to bring her the same drink.

Jane sipped her cocktail. "We also need to celebrate Rachel's news."

Eva raised her eyebrows and glanced at Rachel. "Oh?"

Rachel grinned. "I got the partnership."

Eva stood to hug her. "That's brilliant! Well done, I knew you'd get it. You're the best accountant in that place."

Rachel smiled. "Thank you."

The waiter approached and furnished Eva with her drink. She took her seat again to raise her glass. "To Rachel's partnership."

They clinked glasses.

Jane raised hers towards Eva. "And to Eva."

Rachel stood. "To freedom!"

Eva laughed and took a large swallow of her cocktail.

Rachel took her seat. "What's been happening since you got back?"

Eva screwed up her face.

Rachel raised her eyebrow. "What does that expression mean?"

Eva sighed. "Mum's being sneaky."

Jane frowned. "Sneaky?"

Eva nodded. She turned to Jane. "Her best friend is Damon Evans' mum, Lily. They've been engineering meetings between us."

Rachel laughed. "You mean they're trying to matchmake the two of you because you're both newly single?"

Eva nodded.

Jane smiled. "That's sweet."

"I know," Eva said, "but it's embarrassing. The guy clearly isn't interested. We're going for a drink—but just as friends."

Rachel raised her eyebrow. "And what about you? Are you interested?"

Heat rose in Eva's cheeks. "He's just an old friend."

Rachel studied her for a second, her eyebrow still raised. Eva didn't know why she still had the adolescent tendency to lie about being attracted to someone. It must be an in-built form of self-preservation, to save face when she liked someone who was way out of her league.

Jane was watching Eva's expression. She cleared her throat. "Are you looking forward to starting your new job?"

Eva relaxed again and nodded. "It'll be good to get my teeth into something new. But I'm nervous about it."

Rachel took a sip of her drink. "Do you know anyone who works there?"

Eva shook her head. "But I did meet a few of them when I did my virtual interview, and they all seemed friendly." She sipped her drink and nodded towards Jane. "Did you know that Jane manages the Alton Hall Spa?"

Rachel's eyes widened. "That place looks fantastic. I've still never been, always too busy."

"I can vouch for her skills," Eva said. "I felt brilliant after that hand massage." She rubbed her shoulder. "I think I might book in with you for the back, neck and shoulder version soon."

"Sounds awesome," Rachel sighed. "I'll definitely join you if you're going back." She sipped her drink. "So...we know what's happening with Eva's tragic love life. But are you seeing anyone, Jane?"

Jane darted her gaze over to Eva and appeared to take in Eva's smile. "No, not at the moment. My long-term relationship ended a while back. But it was for the best. I'm young free and single again." She smiled. "Well, young*ish*."

Rachel placed her elbows on the table and touched the ends of her fingers together, a business-like expression on her face. "It is now my mission to find you two a couple of nice men. You each need your very own Marcus."

Eva raised an eyebrow. "I dunno, Rach. I think you struck the jackpot there. He's one in a million."

Rachel shrugged. "We'll just have to search through the next two million to find two more then."

Eva and Jane laughed.

The smile dropped from Rachel's face and she gestured at something behind them.

Eva turned. Tracey McKenna of the teenage-predatory-behaviour-toward-Damon fame was speaking to some guys at the bar. Tracey appeared how Eva would have expected, with the same jet-black hair, thick makeup and a figure-hugging dress that appeared as if she had poured herself into it. Tracey threw her head back and laughed at something the guys were saying.

"Yes," Jane said. "Hard to miss her, isn't it?"

Rachel sipped her drink. "Don't look now but she's coming over here."

A shrill voice called out from behind. "Hi, girlies!"

Eva's heart sank. She gritted her teeth and stood. Tracey approached and threw her arms around Eva, nearly tipping her off balance. Eva steadied the two of them, trying not to inhale too much of the alcohol fumes that Tracey was breathing onto her.

"Eva," Tracey said, pulling back and studying Eva, her face a little too close. "Aw, don't you look...nice."

Tracey released her and kissed Jane's cheek, then she moved towards Rachel, who blocked her attempt at a hug by thrusting her hand out for a shake.

Tracey collapsed into the seat next to Rachel, facing Eva and Jane. "How're you all doing? I've not seen any of you in ages."

There was a brief silence.

"Good, thanks," Jane said. "How're you?"

"Fantastic." Tracey gestured her arm in the air. "I've been doing Weight Watchers since me and Mike split. I've not fit into this dress in about ten years."

Rachel raised her eyebrow and Eva prayed that she wouldn't say anything inappropriate. Eva jumped in, just in case the champagne cocktails had loosened Rachel's liberal tongue further. "You look great. How're you enjoying the single life?"

"Oh it's fab, Evie."

Eva clenched her jaw. She didn't like people she hardly knew using her pet name, especially people like Tracey. She'd always been fake and two-faced, something that Eva had fallen foul of at school.

Tracey studied Eva. "I hear you're newly single too." She paused, barely disguising her intent to elicit signs of misery.

Eva forced a smile. "Yes. I agree with you. It's great."

Tracey didn't do well in hiding her disappointed expression. Her eyes glinted. "It's a shame. From your pictures on social media, Callum was a really good-looking guy. I doubt you'll manage to get one like *him* again."

Rachel frowned and opened her mouth, but Jane interjected. "Tracey, did you hear about the spring school reunion that some of the other girls are organizing?"

Tracey's eyes widened. "Yes, I'm going." She leaned across the table. "I'm hoping Damon will be there. Did you hear that he and Sarah split?"

Rachel's eyes flashed. "You can just ask Eva whether he's going. She and Damon are friends."

Tracey's face fell. "Are you? I didn't realise you were still close.

Eva shot Rachel a look. "No," she said to Tracey, "we aren't really that close."

Tracey's posture relaxed and she fiddled with a coaster. "Are you seeing much of each other?"

Eva cleared her throat. "No.".

Tracey smiled. "Oh, okay." She dropped the coaster back onto the table. "Are you guys going to the reunion?"

Eva glanced at Rachel, who shrugged.

"I'm not sure." Eva said. "I'd forgotten all about it, to be honest."

"It'll be a good laugh," Tracey said. "And you never know. You might meet a man." She stood. "Right, I need another drink. I'm off to the bar to see which lucky guy gets to buy it for me." She turned and walked off, waving her hand above her head in a goodbye.

Eva sank into her chair. She raised her eyebrows at Rachel. "Why did you tell her I was close with Damon? I thought she was going to explode."

"Good," Rachel said. "She was annoying me, the rude cow." She folded her arms and leaned back. "Anyway, you said you and Damon are going for a drink, so you *are* good friends. Unless it *is* something more?"

Eva shook her head. "He's never been interested in me in that way." She took a breath, aware she was speaking too quickly. "In any case, he's still hung up on Sarah. She ended it, not him."

Jane touched Eva's hand. "And what about you? How do *you* feel about *him*?"

Eva hesitated for a second. "I feel the same. I'm not hung up on Callum anymore, but neither am I

45

interested in anyone else." It wasn't a total lie. She *was* over Callum and she wasn't interested in anyone...except for Damon.

Jane watched Eva's face. "Can I ask what happened with Callum?"

Eva glanced up. Rachel was studying her. She'd only given Rachel a brief outline because she was too humiliated to describe any of it out loud. She decided to give Jane the same brief. She cleared her throat. "Let's put it this way. He was more interested in shagging the young secretary from his law firm's office than his wife."

Jane frowned. "That's horrible."

Eva nodded, unable to get any further words out. She lifted her glass and drained it.

"Agreed," Rachel said, watching her. "On that note" — she signalled the waiter — "another round of cocktails."

Chapter Six

The following days dragged for Eva. She was excited to see Damon at the weekend but also terrified. What if she ran out of things to say? What if his handsome looks caused her to lose the power of speech altogether? Or, worst of all, what if he figured out how much she liked him? She didn't want to call Rachel to discuss it because then she'd have to own up about her feelings.

She'd be thirty years old soon and yet she felt like a teenager again. It wasn't just the hormonal lust but also the self-conscious awkwardness, which was strange. It must be the product of life regressing—being cheated on, getting divorced, returning to live with her parents, plus her childhood crush being thrown in her face by her interfering mother.

Eva changed her mind multiple times over the week about what she should wear. She didn't want to appear too understated but neither did she want to be overdressed, because it was merely the local pub they were visiting.

Saturday night loomed and she finally settled on an outfit—another new top courtesy of the 'Meena collection', a fitted T-shirt with stripes alternating blue and gold, navy skinny jeans and ankle-length wedge boots. She decided to team it with a lightweight navy blazer.

The pub was only a mile or so away, not too far from the corner shop, so Eva decided to walk. She gathered her belongings into a handbag and slipped into her boots. "Mum, Dad," she called down the hallway, "I'm going out now."

"Okay," Matthew called back from the living room. "Do you need me to drop you off?"

"No!" said Eva. "I mean, that's okay. I'm just going to walk. We're only going to the Swan."

Meena poked her head round the living room door. "Who're you going with? Rach?"

Eva glanced away. "Yes. That's right." She didn't want them getting the wrong idea—especially Meena, who would have a wedding outfit picked out in five seconds flat.

Meena nodded. "Remember your keys."

Eva opened the door and started sliding out of it. "Yes, Mum."

She closed the door behind her and leaned against it for a moment. Briefly she considered whether this was a bad idea and if she should've cancelled, but it was too late now.

She walked out of the estate and turned along the main road. It struck her how surreal this was. After she met Callum, she'd never dreamed that she'd be back living here.

Lost in her thoughts, she wandered along the path to the pub and paused. She tried to peer inside to see whether Damon was already there, but it was crowded and she couldn't make him out. She walked through the doorway, her pulse quickening with nerves. Maybe she should go to the bar and get a drink to settle her anxiety before he arrived.

She slid into a space at the bar and studied the choices on display.

"Dr. Mathers, I presume?"

She snapped her head to the side at the sound of his voice. Damon was leaning against the bar beside her, the human screen previously between them having drifted away as she'd approached.

Eva's dry mouth took on desert proportions. It was a struggle not to stare at him open-mouthed. He was wearing dark skinny jeans and a fitted black button-down shirt with the top two buttons open and the sleeves rolled up. Eva tried really hard to keep her eyes from the muscles on display in those arms and the glimpse of toned chest at the top of the shirt.

Roughly ten tumbleweeds rolled past in her mind's eye. She forced her voice out of her parched mouth. "Hey." She swallowed in an attempt to lubricate her vocal cords and carefully met his gaze, trying not to give away that she'd just been admiring his physique. "Looking good."

He leaned over and she caught the scent of his aftershave. He'd been right at their first meeting. He did smell gorgeous.

Damon put on a sultry tone. "Why, thank you." He ran a hand through his hair. "It's because I'm worth it." He stared across the bar with a pretend pout, as if he were posing in a catalogue.

Eva laughed, relieved that her tension had dissipated. Good job that it wasn't safe being this close to flammable alcohol when Damon made her heat up to about a million degrees.

He smiled. "What can I get you?"

Eva tried to decide between wine and gin. Then she remembered that the last time she'd drunk wine, she'd ended up telling her Edinburgh friends in great detail how much she loved them all, plus a number of random strangers in the bar. "Gin and tonic, please."

They took their drinks over to a nearby table with two seats across from one another.

Damon held out a chair for her before moving over to sit. "What's going down with you this week?"

Eva wondered how much time he'd spent picking his outfit for tonight. He'd probably thrown on the first thing he'd laid hands on rather than the careful deliberation that she'd gone through. He was as cool as a cucumber.

She sat down and started removing her jacket. "This week I've been mostly worrying about starting my new job and getting the Spanish inquisition from mum, especially about who I'm hanging out with."

He flicked his gaze up to hers. There was a strange look in his eye, but quickly it was gone.

"Oh yeah?" he said. "I've been getting that too from good old Lily. Did you come clean or keep quiet about tonight?"

Eva took a drink. "I lied through my teeth. You?"

"Yeah, me too." He rolled his eyes. "Don't want her breaking out the wedding hat." He sipped his beer and studied her. "Why're you worrying about your job?"

She shrugged. "I always get nervous starting somewhere new, all the different processes and pathways to learn. I don't like being inefficient and it'll take a while to get up to speed." Something work-related niggled at the back of her mind but she deliberately didn't let it drift into the forefront. It was something she was careful not to think about.

"I'm sure you'll settle in quickly," Damon said.

She smiled, deciding it best to change the subject in case he probed further. "How's your work going?"

"Great," he said. "We've gotten some lucrative new contracts and moved to a larger office."

"That's brilliant," she said. "I'm glad things are going well."

As the evening went on, it occurred to Eva that being with Damon wasn't awkward at all. The conversation flowed easily and his company relaxed her. True, she was mesmerized by his mouth when he was speaking, thinking for the millionth time how it might feel to kiss it. But hopefully he didn't notice.

She smiled. "How're your kids doing?"

Damon's eyes lit up. "Great thanks. Adele's right into that new girl band."

Eva laughed. "You mean The Go Girls? Rachel's daughters love them too."

He grinned. "Yeah, that's them. She's got all the merchandise and Sarah's going to get tickets for a live show when they go on sale."

Eva watched him carefully as he mentioned Sarah's name but didn't see any sign of emotion register on his face. *He must be a good actor.* "How old's Adele now? Six?"

Damon smiled. "That's right. And Sam's three."

Eva took a drink. "What's he into?"

Damon laughed. "Everything he shouldn't be. He likes climbing, so I have to watch him like a hawk."

It crossed Eva's mind how difficult it must be for a father not to live full time with his family anymore. He'd brought them up from birth but now he wouldn't get to see them every morning and tuck them into bed every night. "Did you have them last weekend?"

Damon nodded. "We went out to pick wallpaper for their new rooms at my place." He spun a coaster on the table. "I really miss them, you know." He glanced up. "I know it sounds weird me saying that when I've just been talking about spending time with them."

She shook her head. "Not at all. It must be difficult for you not living with them and Sarah."

Damon seemed far away for a moment. He must have been thinking about how he missed Sarah and wanted her back. "Yes, it is. Really difficult."

Eva touched his hand. "Would it be better to do one of those exact fifty-fifty arrangements? I know people who have their kids four days one week then three the next."

He smiled. "We discussed it, but we felt it'd be better for them to have a stable home during the week. And Sarah's happy for me to have the lion's share of the weekends to make up for it."

Eva nodded.

"Anyway," he said, spinning his coaster, "you'd better get your violin out, the way this conversation's going."

Eva raised her eyebrows. "I actually used to play the violin at school, remember? There's no way you'd want me to get that out, unless you wanted your ears to start bleeding."

"Oh yeah, I forgot about that." Damon said. "You were really good." He nodded earnestly then as she glanced away, he shook his head firmly and made a 'yikes' expression, clearly knowing full well that she could still see him from the corner of her eye. She looked back at his face and he started nodding again.

Eva laughed. "Don't push your luck, Evans. Seriously though, you can talk to me about anything, including the sad stuff. I even promise not to get the violin out."

He studied her intently. "Thanks. I appreciate that." He grinned. "Especially the bit about the violin." He rubbed at his ears with a pained expression.

Eva rolled her eyes, smiling. She pushed her chair back. "I'll be back in a sec." She stood to head for the ladies' room.

When she came back out, she gestured to Damon to indicate she was going to the bar and mouthed 'same again?' He gave her a thumbs-up.

After ordering, she returned to the table and passed him his beer. "There you go. Don't say I never give you anything."

"Thanks," Damon said. "Let me know if there's anything else on offer."

She caught his gaze and he winked at her, lifting his bottle and taking a sip.

Eva's stomach tumbled. So, what was that comment meant to mean? Another throwaway Damon flirtation? Or was there a possibility he did find her attractive? She just couldn't tell.

She cleared her throat. "Did you hear about the reunion?"

He nodded. "Are you going?"

She sipped her gin and tonic. "I'm not sure. Rachel and Jane want to. What about you?"

He shrugged. "Maybe. Some of the other guys are going, so it could be a laugh."

Eva nodded. "I think I'm hesitant because school wasn't much fun for me. I wasn't bullied or anything, but I did feel pretty marginalized" — she smiled — "for being a massive square, obviously."

Damon flashed a grin. "Don't forget also being a speccy four-eyes."

Eva punched his arm lightly. "Thin ice, Evans."

He grinned more widely then stuck out his bottom lip and rubbed his arm, looking at her with puppy-dog eyes. "You always did pack a punch. I was on the receiving end of a few of those at school. Even when we played 'kiss catch', you still used to punch me instead of kiss me."

There's no way I'd make that mistake again. Eva raised her eyebrow. "That's all you deserved." She leaned back, smiling.

"True," Damon said. "I was a very naughty boy."

A shiver shot up Eva's spine as thoughts regarding how naughty Damon might be came tumbling into her mind. He caught her eye, but this time there was no wink.

He leaned towards her. "Seriously, though. I didn't know you felt that way at school. Marginalized, I mean. You never told me that."

Eva looked at him. "It wasn't the sort of thing we would've discussed. We didn't speak much at high school, did we?" She smiled. "Anyway, you were part of the popular gang, so I didn't think you'd be concerned about the plight of us unpopular sorts."

He frowned. "You weren't *unpopular*, Eva."

She laughed. "Yeah I was. You don't have to be polite. I know that having a brain and wearing glasses wasn't sexy."

He raised his eyebrow. "Says who?"

Eva's heart rate sped up. She cleared her throat. "Eric Donovan for one. He asked me out and I said I'd think about it. Then he and his mates started laughing at me. He said it'd only been a joke, that there was no way he'd want to go out with the least sexy girl in the school."

Damon's expression soured. "What an arsehole. Don't tell me you took that idiot's opinion to heart?"

Eva shrugged.

Damon frowned. "Did you even like him?"

She shook her head and averted her eyes. "No. I always thought he was a bit of a twat."

Damon ducked his head a little, making her gaze meet his again. "It didn't matter what he thought then, did it?"

Eva swallowed. Why did this even bother her over a decade later? "I guess not."

"I reckon," Damon said, "that the only reason he said that was because he lost face when you said you'd think about it. You didn't say yes straight away."

Eva frowned, unconvinced.

"Anyway," he said, "his fragile masculinity was never any of your concern and you shouldn't let that affect your decision about going to the reunion. The guy was a dick, and it was years ago."

Eva nodded. "I know. It's just something I've always remembered because it was so humiliating."

Damon clenched his jaw. "I wish I'd been there. I would've wiped the smile off his face." He paused, fiddling with the label on his beer bottle. "I did miss you, you know."

Eva frowned. "What do you mean?"

"After we started hanging around with different people at school," he said. "I missed having you as a friend."

She smiled. He'd missed her as friend, which was lovely and filled her with a warm glow. But he'd never longed for her the way she had for him. She started to feel nervous that she might say something to give that away if they carried on talking about the subject for much longer. She took a deep breath and glanced at her watch. Time had flown. "I'd better head back or Mum'll have the search party out for me."

Damon looked at his own watch. "Wow, I didn't realise the time. You have tantalized me for too long, Dr. Mathers."

Eva gathered her jacket and they headed for the exit. Damon held the door for her. She caught his scent and her pulse quickened.

"Do you want me to walk you back to yours?" Damon asked.

She shook her head. "That's okay. It's out of your way. Anyhow, I'll be fine. It's only two minutes more from where I leave you." Eva was nervous that him walking her to the door might feel awkward. She'd be dying to kiss him and he might get that something was up.

"Sure?"

"Yeah. I've always got my super punch if needed."

They soon approached the crossroads where they'd part company. Eva tended to hug her friends goodbye, but as they drew to a stop, she suffered an internal struggle about whether to do that or not. There was a real risk she might burst into flames at the sensation of being hugged by Damon. But then it'd be awkward if she just waved at him or shook his hand.

Damon smiled. "I really enjoyed that. Fancy hanging out another time if you're free?"

"Yes, absolutely." She cleared her throat. "I mean. I'd like that." She hoped that he wouldn't read into her enthusiasm and guess correctly regarding her feelings. Eva hesitated, still unsure whether to just walk off or not. Then the parting gesture was decided for her when Damon enveloped her in a bear hug, lifting her off the ground. It was done in a jokey manner, but every fibre of her being was shocked into heightened awareness. She was conscious of the press of his chest, the feel of his hard thighs against her legs, the smell of him...

Then he set her down and waved as he moved away. "Text me when you get back so I know you're home safe." He grinned. "Or 'face-chat', if you prefer."

Eva waved and turned away. She drifted home, remembering the feel of him against her.

Once back, she started analysing everything he'd said and done to try to find some shred of evidence that he might find her attractive, even just a little bit. But there was nothing concrete at all.

Chapter Seven

The next day Eva had to make a concerted effort not to obsess over Damon. She'd gone over and over everything he'd said and done the night before and was driving herself mad with it. After she'd texted him to say she was home safe, he'd messaged back to say goodnight and to let her know when he was free to meet again.

She concluded that it meant the ball was now firmly in her court. But she couldn't text too soon or he might think her too eager — which she was, but he mustn't know that.

So she resolved to hold out until the next weekend before texting him. He'd have the kids then anyway, so he probably wouldn't be free until the week after.

To take her mind off it, she video-called Rachel.

Rachel connected. "Hey. How did your non-date with Damon go?"

Eva hesitated. She needed to describe it without giving away how she felt. "Fine. It was really nice to catch up. He told me about how the kids were getting on and stuff."

Rachel sighed and rolled her eyes. "At any point did you tell him that you used to be madly in love with him at school and you still fancy the arse off him now?"

Eva stared open-mouthed. "What do you mean?"

Rachel waved her hand. "Don't play all coy. It's me, your best bud. I could tell you were head over heels with him at school. It was written all over your face in history class. And I know you really like him now."

Eva put her head in her hand. "Oh God. If you can tell, that means he can too."

Rachel smiled. "Don't be daft. Firstly, it's not embarrassing. He should be over the moon that someone as hot as you fancies him. Secondly, I doubt he can tell, because men are really dense about these things."

Eva frowned. "Are they? I don't think Callum was."

Rachel shook her head. "That's because he was cocky. No offence."

Eva shrugged. "None taken."

"I reckon it's a good sign about a man," Rachel continued. "If he finds it hard to tell when a woman likes him, it means he doesn't have an over-inflated ego and doesn't think any female who passes him the time of day must be dying to jump his bones."

Eva nodded. "I suppose you've got a point."

Rachel smiled. "Marcus had no clue, bless him. He thought I just wanted to be friends. I practically had to stand in front of him in my underwear to make the point."

Eva sniggered at the thought of a puzzled Marcus with Rachel in her skimpy undies, hands on hips, a frown on her face. She stopped laughing. "Oh no, now I've just imagined you in your underwear. Weird."

Rachel laughed. "You've seen me in my underwear before, you dunce."

Eva smiled. "Oh yeah. And very nice you looked too." Something occurred to her. "Hey, do you reckon Jane suspects I like Damon?"

Rachel nodded. "I think so."

Eva groaned.

"Stop being a wimp," Rachel said. "There's nothing to be ashamed of. He's a really nice, handsome, funny guy and you're both single."

Eva screwed up her face. "He's also way out of my league."

Rachel shook her head. "For goodness sake. We aren't at school anymore. The ridiculous pigeonholing of people no longer applies. You're gorgeous and have everything going for you. You're hilarious, though not as funny as me, obviously." Rachel grinned. "And you're clever and successful. Men are always falling over themselves for you, but you just don't notice because your self-esteem needs a boost."

Eva laughed, but the last part struck a chord. Her self-esteem *had* taken a huge knock at school, and while it had blossomed to a degree through university, after the whole Callum debacle it was now at low ebb. When she thought about it she understood that her whole relationship with Callum had worn away her confidence.

However, there was no way she could bring herself to think that she was on a level playing field with Damon. She'd had him on a pedestal for too long.

Eva felt foolish realizing that her friends had known but she hadn't had the courage to speak to them about it. So, the next time she saw Jane, Eva decided she'd confess to her as well.

* * * *

Jane opened the spa café menu. "What do you fancy to eat? The open sandwiches are really tasty here."

"Sounds great," Eva said.

Jane looked up. "Not long now until you start your new job. Have you been making the most of your time off?"

Eva nodded. "I've been spending time with my mum and trying not to succumb to tea poisoning."

Jane laughed. "Pardon?"

Eva rolled her eyes. "She's some sort of tea addict. She's always been the same. She even has a cup of tea with a hot dinner."

Jane smiled. "She sounds sweet. Oh, how was your drink with Damon?"

"Good." Eva nodded. "Although…"

Jane sipped her coffee. "Although what?"

Eva met Jane's gaze. "Nothing romantic happened."

Jane raised her eyebrows. "But you'd hoped something might?"

Eva screwed up her face. "Stupid, I know."

Jane shook her head. "Not at all. Did you tell him that you want to be more than friends?"

Eva frowned. "No. He definitely doesn't see me that way."

"How do you know if you don't speak to him about it?" Jane said. "In any case, I can't see why he wouldn't reciprocate. You get on great and it sounds like there's chemistry."

The idea of telling Damon how she felt about him made Eva feel sick, so she changed the subject. "Enough about me. How's your love life going?"

Jane rolled her eyes. "Rubbish. I haven't been on any good dates lately. I'm trying some of these dating apps, but I find it all a bit odd. Some of the guys' profile pictures are quite explicit."

Eva raised her eyebrows. "Really?"

Jane blew out her breath through pursed lips. "Yes, like you wouldn't believe. Not the shy and retiring types... And flashy sorts—or flash*ing* sorts, for that matter—aren't really my thing."

Eva choked on her water. "I don't blame you."

Jane stared into the middle distance. "Although..."

Eva frowned. "What?"

Jane flicked her gaze back to meet Eva's. "Do you remember Dave?"

Eva nodded. "Dave Hopewell, from school?"

Jane smiled. "That's right. I ended up bumping into him the other day and we got chatting. He said he was going to the reunion."

Eva thought for a moment. "Oh yeah, that's right. Damon is friends with Dave and he mentioned that the guys were going."

"Dave's single too," Jane said. "I used to really like him at school and he's still really cute and funny. Then when I told him I might be going to the reunion, he looked pleased."

Eva smiled. "That's great."

Jane cleared her throat. "The only thing is I'm nervous to go on my own. The friends I've kept in touch with from school aren't going. Do you think you and Rachel and Marcus will come and we can all go together?"

Eva hesitated. "I'm not sure it's going to be my thing. I think I'm already in touch with all the people I want to be from school."

Jane appeared flattered, but then stared pleadingly into Eva's eyes.

Eva sighed. "Oh, okay. But if you get off with Dave, and Rachel and Marcus are snogging in a corner with me playing gooseberry, then I'm off."

Jane hugged Eva over the table. "It's going to be so much fun."

"Yeah right," said Eva. "As much fun as sticking pins in my eyes."

Jane smiled. "Oh, come on. You might end up snogging someone in a corner yourself. Someone called Damon, maybe?"

"Ha," said Eva. "Like he'd be interested. Even if he was, I'd have to fight Tracey McKenna off first."

Jane shook her head. "No way she has a chance next to you. And I reckon she knows it." She frowned. "That's why she was trying to dress you down at drinks the other night."

Eva shrugged. "Whatever. She's welcome to have a go at him. He's still in love with Sarah anyway."

On Saturday morning, to keep her mind off her temptation to message Damon too soon after their 'date', Eva decided to drive to the nearby lake and have a walk. It was a lovely Spring day and she hadn't been there in ages. She could do with some fresh air and it'd be good to see the place, having enjoyed it so much as a kid. She wondered if Rachel's girls went there much. It was a nice, gentle walk and there was a play park nearby. She resolved to ask Rachel about it and whether they might take the girls one weekend. She enjoyed seeing children having fun. Having kids was something she and Callum had talked about doing when they got into their thirties, but he'd ended up 'doing' Hannah from work instead.

The drive over the hills towards the lake was beautiful. The sun was bright in the sky and the interior of the car quickly became warm. Eva wound down the window and let the wind tousle her hair. She pulled into the car park and watched the sun glint over the lake. It appeared placid and still. Eva was strangely envious. She wished she felt as calm as those waters.

She started off on the walk around the water's edge, alone with her thoughts. Callum had been trespassing in her mind less and less often nowadays, but today was one of those days that he'd found his way in.

'I have to work late again tonight, Eva. I'll be home when I can.'

Work indeed. Eva thought about their relationship and how with hindsight they weren't right for each other. Yet she'd been utterly convinced of their compatibility at the time. *How come?* She was supposed to be intelligent. *Love definitely is blind.* It must've been something to do with her disbelief that someone as charismatic as him would be interested in her. He'd flattered her low self-confidence and she'd been suckered in.

Before she knew it, she was most of the way around the small lake and she spotted a familiar bench at the water's edge. She crossed the path to sit for a moment. There were some ducks on the lake, sending out little ripples across the surface. She watched the small waves gather momentum and move out across the water, thinking back to Callum and the crescendo of the end of their relationship.

'It's okay, hon. We'll talk about it tomorrow. Don't worry. It'll be fine.'

Tomorrow never came with Callum.

Another voice unexpectedly appeared in her head, a female one that she'd become adept at blocking out.

'It'll be all right, won't it, Eva? We've caught it in time?'

The hairs on the back of her neck stood up and nausea washed over her. She was normally good at preventing that memory from surfacing, but for some reason, today her subconscious was vulnerable. She took a deep breath and pushed the voice to the back of her mind.

The sound of a family approaching around the corner became apparent, so she pulled herself together lest a bunch of strangers see her break down in public. She looked up then realised they weren't strangers. Her heart rose.

"Yes, Adele, we can feed the ducks now. Have you got the seed? Sam, watch your step. It's muddy there." Damon glanced over and did a double-take. Then he smiled and waved.

She stood and walked over, giving him a brief peck on the cheek and using all her willpower not to look at his lips, never mind kiss too near them. Even still, the fire burned as she grazed his cheek gently. "Hi."

She crouched to greet the kids. "Hey, Adele. Hey, Sam. Long time, no see. Remember me? I saw you last year when I stopped by to visit your grandma."

Adele shook her head. Sam seemed more interested in quacking at the ducks.

"This is my friend Eva," Damon said. "She's Auntie Meena's daughter."

Adele shrugged.

"That's okay if you don't remember," Eva said. "You know what I remember though? That you like The Go Girls. Who's your favourite?"

Adele's eyes widened. "I like Amelia the best. She has the same hair as me." She lifted her dark hair.

Eva nodded. "You're right. You have exactly the same hair. I like Amelia too. She's the best singer."

Adele nodded. "Mummy's got us tickets to go and see them. I'm going to dress like Amelia, and Mummy will be Sophia, cause they have the same yellow hair and their names begin with the same letter."

Eva smiled. "It's really clever that you know that. You must be good at spelling. You and your mummy will have loads of fun at the concert. I wish I were going. I bet they sing my favourite one, *Girls Rock*." Eva made a rock sign with her hand and pretended to head-bang.

Adele giggled. "I love that one."

Eva glanced up and spotted Damon smiling at them as he took out a bag of bird feed at the water's edge and handed some to Sam.

Sam threw some feed onto the water. "Quack, quack, duckies."

"That's right, Sam, quack, quack," Damon said.

Adele took some of the feed, tossing a sprinkling to the ducks and passing Eva a handful.

Eva scattered her feed onto the water. "You know Adele, your dad and I used to come here during the school holidays to learn water sports."

Adele opened her mouth. "Did you? Daddy, can you surf?"

Damon laughed. "It wasn't that sort of water sport. There isn't any surf on a lake, sweet pea. We did boating and canoeing."

Eva frowned. "Except I missed the last couple of days because I broke my foot."

"How did you do that?" Adele asked.

"I walked into a chair."

Damon laughed. "I forgot about that."

"Hey," Eva said, smiling, "it was really sore."

"Yeah, Dad, shut up," said Adele.

"Hey, stop ganging up on me," Damon said, grinning at Eva.

They used up the last of the feed then wandered along the path towards the car park. Adele and Sam ran ahead, playing catch along the way.

"Do you guys come here a lot? I used to love it as a kid," Eva said.

"Yes, when the weather's nice," he replied. "I'd forgotten all about that summer activity club we did. Once they're old enough, I'll need to enrol them in that." His face fell. "I suppose Sarah will want to take care of all that now."

Eva's heart ached for him. She reached round to his opposite shoulder and tugged him towards her. "You'll still be equally involved. I'll bet Sarah will make sure of it."

He glanced at her and smiled. "Yeah, you're right. Thank you."

She smiled back and squeezed his shoulders briefly before letting go. She could feel the strength of his muscular shoulder under her hand and she didn't want to overexcite herself again.

The four of them entered the car park and the children picked their way along the edge to the play area. Eva watched Adele help Sam onto the small climbing frame.

"They're like you and your sister," Eva said.

He smiled and nodded.

Eva turned to him. "What're you doing the rest of the weekend?"

He flicked his hair out of his eyes and she resisted the urge to brush it away for him. "We're going to lunch today with my mum and dad, then tomorrow I'm taking them to the cinema. After that, I'm dropping them back at Sarah's and meeting Dave at the pub." He rolled his eyes. "Now that he's single as well, he keeps talking about us going out to score women. He says we can be others' wingman."

Eva laughed. "Cheesy."

"Tell me about it." Damon shook his head. "Truth is I'm not interested in all that."

"Nah, me neither," Eva said. "I mean scoring guys, not women."

Damon's raised his eyebrows. "You mean you *are* interested in scoring women? Awesome."

Eva shook her head at him, smiling. There was only one person she was interested in.

She wondered if she should ask whether Dave had mentioned Jane, but she didn't want to break her friend's confidence, so she decided to wait and check with Jane first. She could always ask Damon another time. She really hoped that there'd be another time.

Eva wanted to mention meeting again, but she couldn't quite muster the words. Was it appropriate when they'd just been talking about trying to score? And after he'd said he wasn't interested in dating anyone, no doubt due to his on going feelings for Sarah. Was he throwing her a gentle hint that he didn't want to meet?

It seemed as though the moment to speak up had passed. "I'll let you get back to the kids. See you later."

He smiled. "See you."

She walked to her car, disappointed in her lack of courage. There was a shout and she turned towards it. Adele and Sam were waving from the top of the climbing frame. She waved back.

Damon looked over as he headed towards the kids. "Hey, Mathers!"

"What?" she called back.

He imitated holding a phone to his ear. "Call me!"

Eva gave a thumbs-up and got into her car, feeling hopeful once more.

Chapter Eight

The next evening Damon showered before going out to meet Dave at the Swan. He pushed his face under the hot water, hoping it might wash away the thoughts of Eva going round in his head. He remembered the moment he spotted her at the lake the previous day. The sun had glinted off her dark hair, revealing tints of red that sparkled like tiny rubies. She'd been dressed casually in jeans, a loose vest top and a thin cardigan, but she'd still looked amazing. The feel of her arm around his shoulders was awesome and she even smelled great.

Damon reached through the water and turned the shower heat down a few notches, trying to quench his feelings of desire. It was a losing battle.

After he finished and towelled off, he pulled on some jeans and a jumper that were closest to hand. It was a much quicker decision than last weekend when he'd gone to meet Eva. He must've tried on about five different shirts before settling on one. He gathered his wallet and keys and left for the pub.

He arrived roughly ten minutes after the time they'd arranged, but Dave wasn't there yet. Damon headed to the bar to get them a couple of pints then found a table in the corner. Dave arrived just as he sat down. Damon smiled. Dave had a habit of arriving after a drink had been bought and was ready for him.

Dave took a seat. "All right, Damo? How goes it?"

"Good, thanks." Damon pushed one of the drinks across the table. "That's for you."

"Ah, thanks, man. You're a pal."

Damon smiled. "How's work?"

Dave nodded. "Great. We're building an extension in that posh estate, the ones where the houses have names instead of numbers."

Damon frowned. "I thought you'd finished that one?"

Dave took a gulp of his pint. "We did. This is across the road from the last one."

Damon raised his eyebrows. "You've obviously made a name for yourself in that area."

Dave grinned. "It's a domino effect, like a keeping up with the Joneses thing. They see what someone else is getting done and don't want to be outshone. Snobby really, but it works for us."

Damon laughed. "I'm pretty sure it's got a lot to do with the quality of your work. Don't you think?"

Dave shrugged. "Speaking of snobbery, did you say you were out with Eva Mathers the other week?"

Damon frowned. "Yeah. What do you mean about snobbery?"

Dave took another slug of his beer. "She was a bit aloof at school, wasn't she? High and mighty and no time to speak to the likes of us."

Damon shook his head. "She was quiet, and I'm sure she thought we were a couple of jokers. But you didn't know her as well as I did. She was just shy back then. She's really cool and funny. I reckon you two would get on well."

Dave eyed him over the rim of his pint glass. "What's happening with you guys then?"

Damon sipped his drink. "Nothing, we're just mates. She's not long broken up with her husband."

Dave pursed his lips. "Is she coming to the reunion?"

Damon fiddled with a coaster. "Not sure."

"I'm keen to go," Dave said. He clinked his glass against Damon's. "And I reckon you should come too."

Damon met his gaze. "What makes you so keen?"

Dave hesitated. "Did I tell you I saw Jane Whitely the other day?"

Damon shook his head.

Dave took a breath. "She's single now. She looked gorgeous."

Damon smiled. "You had a real crush on her at school."

Dave drained more of his drink. "Oh boy, totally. Never did anything about it, though, because I was too much of a wimp. I figure this might be my second chance."

Damon grinned. "You've abandoned the 'going out on the score' idea then?"

Dave laughed. "I reckon I'm too old for all that crap anyway. But I'm definitely interested in Jane."

Damon eyed him, empathic to his situation. Maybe he couldn't have the person he really wanted, but Dave might be in with a chance, so he'd do everything he could to support him. "Yeah okay. Let's go to the reunion. It'll be a laugh."

"Brilliant." Dave raised his pint glass to clink it against Damon's. "Cheers. Now we just need to find you a woman. Maybe Eva? I'll see if I can work my wingman magic on her at the reunion."

Damon pulled his glass from his lips. "No way." He shook his head. "You'll scare her off. In any case, she's still out of my league. She's a brainy doctor and bloody gorgeous. Plus, she's just been jilted and is still in love with her ex-husband."

Dave raised an eyebrow. "Maybe just some hot and heavy sessions then?"

Damon coughed on his beer. "I don't think she'd be up for that either."

Dave shook his head. "You would be, though. You're going to explode if you don't get some action soon. Separate rooms for the past year with Sarah and no other women on the scene? It's not good for a guy. I'm going to help you with that." He grinned. "By finding you a woman of course. You're not *that* good a mate."

Damon sighed and rolled his eyes. "Whatever you say." Something occurred to him. "Actually, I think Eva is friends with Jane. Do you want me to sound it out for you?"

Dave hesitated. "Maybe. It'd need to be subtle. Don't say I was obsessed with her at school or anything, or she'll think I'm some sort of crazy stalker and be running for the hills."

Damon shook his head, his face straight. "Don't worry. I won't tell Eva that." He paused. "I'll just tell her that you've got a shrine to Jane built in your bedroom and that you masturbate furiously over it every night."

Dave started coughing on his drink and ended up spraying beer across the table. He cleared his throat and gave Damon a hard stare. "Watch it, Evans, or else I'm going to have to start advertising for a new wingman."

When Damon returned home, he spent the rest of the evening repeatedly checking his phone for messages from Eva. He'd been hoping she would've texted by now about them seeing each other again.

Chapter Nine

Eva studied her cornflakes. She was too nervous to eat. Instead she sipped at her coffee, not registering what her mother was saying.

"So I told them no way," Meena said. "What do you think, Eva?"

Eva fiddled with her spoon. "Yeah, Mum, definitely."

Meena eyed her from across the table. "Nervous, *beti*?"

Eva glanced up from the contours of her cornflakes. "Yeah. A bit."

Meena touched her hand. "Don't worry. It'll all fall into place."

Eva nodded.

Meena squeezed her hand. "The thought of it is worse than the reality. And if any bad memories resurface, you can talk to me and your dad."

Eva smiled. "I know, thanks." She got up from the table, in case Meena tried to speak any further. "I think once today is out of the way, it'll be fine."

She headed for the door, deciding to set off early. She might as well get there and make a start rather than sitting at home feeling nervous.

As she opened the door to leave, Meena came hurrying down the hallway carrying a large butter container. "Here, *beti*. Take these sweets in for the staff at the surgery. Everyone loves *mithai*."

Eva smiled as she opened it and smelled the Pakistani delicacies. Her mum always kept old butter tubs to fill with sweet treats. She kissed her cheek. "Thanks. I'm sure they'll love them."

When she arrived at the practice and parked, she admired the view over the river. She watched the swans. They seemed to be gliding effortlessly, but under the water their legs would be kicking furiously. That was how she felt sometimes.

Her first day went well, though she was pretty much run off her feet. By the time she left the surgery, Emma the receptionist was locking up. Emma passed her Meena's empty butter container. "Those were lovely. Tell your mum we're happy to take any surplus baking she has."

Eva smiled. "I'll tell her. She'll love that." She waved goodbye and got into her car, her head buzzing with all the information she'd absorbed during the day. She drove home, chatted to her mum and updated her about the popularity of the *mithai*. After dinner she decided to reward herself by messaging Damon.

Hey. How're you?

Good, thanks. How was your first day?

It went well, thanks. Just wondering if you want to meet up at the weekend?

Definitely. Fancy the cinema?

Sounds awesome.

Great. How about Sunday?

You're on.

Eva sighed with relief. *See now, that wasn't too hard, was it?* She tried to stop herself imagining being in a dimly lit movie theatre with Damon and him leaning over to take her hand then kissing her…

* * * *

Eva's first week at work went well and she felt she was finding her feet quickly. On Saturday morning, she decided to go for a run. She hadn't been exercising much lately and had decided that she needed to look after herself better.

She changed into her running gear and tried to decide whether to attach her iPod or her phone to her arm. She opted for the iPod because it had more charge.

Eva started off at a steady pace. Hopefully she might manage five kilometres if she took it slowly. She might have to run a bit and walk a bit, but that was okay. She quickly got into a rhythm and two kilometres in found it wasn't as hard as she thought it was going to be.

She cranked up the dance music she liked to listen to while running. The bass kicked in, giving her a rush of adrenaline. She started going faster, feeling empowered. Her adrenaline and the bass in the song made her fantasize about kicking Callum's ass.

Boom

She imagined herself punching Callum in the face.

Boom

She drop-kicked Hannah to the ground.

Boom

Pain exploded in her leg. "Shit! Oww!" The bottom of her right calf burned with agony. It sent her into a hop before she managed to stop and balance against a low wall. She tried to put weight on it but could barely manage a hobble, so she sat on the wall and looked around. No one was nearby. The blow to her leg felt as if someone had thrown something. Then it dawned on her. It hadn't been an impact. She'd been taking it too fast too soon and her Achilles tendon had gone.

Great. Now what? There was no way she could manage to hop back home, especially up the hill she'd just come down. And her genius idea to bring her iPod instead of her phone was an epic fail.

Eva glanced along the road and figured out that she wasn't far from Damon's, plus it wasn't uphill to get there. If she made it, then she could use his phone to call her mum and dad. They were out shopping but it wouldn't take them long to come get her. She gritted her teeth and hobbled off in the direction of Damon's.

* * * *

Damon finished straightening the living room and glanced around, trying to think if he'd forgotten anything before he went out. Adele and Sam would be arriving soon after his return so he wanted everything ready. The doorbell rang. *Must be the postman.* He went into the hallway and pulled open the door. His eyes widened at the sight of at Eva in her running gear, panting and glistening with sweat. Electricity shocked through him, then he registered the pained expression on her face and the fact that she was standing on one leg and propping herself against the doorframe. Anxiety rose in his gut. He frowned. "Are you okay?"

She took a deep breath. "Not really. I'm so sorry to turn up like this, but I was running and I've knackered my leg. The kids aren't here yet, are they?"

Damon shook his head. "Come on. I'll help you in." He steadied her by putting his arm around her waist and supported her into the house, through the living room door and onto the sofa.

He crouched in front of her. "Let's have a look." He carefully ran his hands along the back of her leg. "It's your lower calf, isn't it? It feels swollen." Damon gently let go, his heart racing at the touch of her skin. He reminded himself that Eva was in pain and this wasn't the time to be getting overexcited.

Eva frowned. "I'm worried I've ruptured my Achilles tendon."

Damon screwed up his face. "Ouch."

She sighed. "Could I borrow your phone? I'm going to have to call Mum and Dad to take me to Accident and Emergency."

"Of course." He passed her his mobile. "I'm going to get you an ice pack." He entered the kitchen, and as he rummaged around in the freezer, he heard Eva leave her parents a voicemail on each of their mobiles. She cursed under her breath. Damon wrapped the ice pack in a tea towel.

He came back through and crouched in front of her, placing the ice pack on the back of her calf.

She winced. "Thank you."

He met her gaze. "No luck getting hold of them?"

"No." She rubbed her temples. "What's the point of having a mobile phone if it's switched off all the bloody time?"

He smiled. "My parents are the same." He touched her hand. "Listen... I can drive you to A&E. It's no problem."

She shook her head. "I feel bad enough dropping in on you like this."

He took her hand and squeezed it. "You need to get this sorted. I'm not picking the kids up till dinner time."

"Are you sure?" She squeezed his hand back. "You don't have anywhere to be just now?"

"Nope." He stood from his crouching position. "Let me get my wallet and keys from the kitchen and we'll go."

He went through, grabbed the items and quickly tapped out a text on his phone, cancelling his lunch plans out of sight. He went back into the living room. "Come on then, wounded soldier." He lifted her to her feet. She tried to walk and yelped.

The pain in her voice was like a knife to his gut. "Nope," he said. "We're not doing that." He hauled her into his arms.

Eva smiled weakly. "You're going to do your back in, then we'll both need to be driven to the hospital."

He smiled. "Don't worry. I'm big and tough. I've been working out. Once we get there, remind me to show you my guns." He walked towards the door and managed to open it one-handed, then carried her out onto the driveway. He set her down carefully by the passenger side of his car then helped her in before going back to shut and lock the front door.

Damon got into the car and they set off for the hospital. His phone buzzed in his pocket, no doubt Dave calling to ask why he'd cancelled on him at the last minute. But he'd make it up to him another time.

Chapter Ten

Eva smiled with relief when the local hospital came into view. After they parked, Damon insisted on carrying her to the front door, where he proceeded to support her through the revolving doors to reception and she booked in. They moved over to the seating area. Luckily, it wasn't too busy.

Eva settled into the plastic chair. "Listen… You don't need to stay with me. You go and get on with your day. Mum and Dad are bound to turn on their phones soon and I can get them to come collect me."

Damon leaned back in his seat. "No way. I'm staying here. I want to see all the emergency room action like on TV." He winked. "Anyway, I've not shown you my biceps yet."

Eva smiled. There he went again. Flirtatious comments falling from his lovely mouth like confetti. But was there anything behind them? She was in too much pain to overanalyse, so she was just going to enjoy his attention. She pretended to roll her eyes. "Go on then. Let's see these guns."

Damon rolled up his sleeve and flexed his muscles.

Eva shrugged, trying to play down her enthusiasm. "Oh yeah, not bad." She lifted her hand and placed it on his arm, giving it a squeeze then immediately regretting it, because her heart sped up to dangerous levels. She was pretty sure that everyone in the waiting room would be able to hear it beating like a drum.

Damon was doing his mock pout again. She laughed and inadvertently set her foot onto the floor, resulting in the laugh morphing into a moan of pain.

"Oops," Damon said. "The gun show is too much for some."

Eva leaned back into her chair and sighed.

Damon put his arm around her shoulders.

She looked at him. "This is just my bloody luck, isn't it?"

He gave her shoulders a squeeze, then raised his hand to her cheek, stroking lightly down to her jawline. She closed her eyes for a second, revelling in his touch. When she opened them again, something had shifted in his gaze. What was it? He didn't drop his fingers for another tantalizing couple of seconds. He smiled then pulled her into a hug. Eva decided just to absorb it and not overthink for a change. She leaned into him and rested her head on his shoulder. Damon played with her ponytail.

"Sorry I'm sweaty and gross," she said into his shoulder. "You'll need a second shower after touching me."

"Don't worry." The bass of his voice vibrated against her cheek. "I like the feel of your sweaty body against mine."

Excitement rippled through her. She didn't dare look up in case he gave her that jokey wink, which she always took to mean 'just kidding'.

Instead, she nestled in closer and he rested his chin on top of her head. She was in pain and she was going to allow herself this small pleasure. Just this once she going to let herself believe there was something in it.

He continued to stroke her hair and reached his other hand to take hers, rubbing his thumb over the back of it. Eva thought she going to go into pleasure overload. Every nerve ending was tingling, every hair standing on end and there was a fire burning in her pelvis. The only spoiler was the dull throb in her right calf, but even that dimmed into insignificance at Damon's touch.

Eva was disappointed when the triage nurse called her name. She extricated herself from Damon's side and he supported her to go through to the nurse's office. He stopped at the door. She glanced back at him and reached out. "Will you come with me?"

He took her hand and followed her into the room.

The nurse asked some questions and did some basic observations. Then she collected a wheelchair and pushed Eva along the corridor to one of the cubicles. "The doctor will be with you soon. Can I get you or your boyfriend a drink of water?"

Eva was in too much pain to correct the nurse. "No thank you."

Damon shook his head. "I'm fine, thanks."

Eva waited for Damon to rectify the misunderstanding about him being her boyfriend but he didn't.

The nurse left the cubicle and drew the curtain over.

Damon took a seat next to Eva. She stared at the floor, still terrified he was going to put their close encounter in the waiting room into the friendship context. But he didn't say anything. He just shifted his chair closer and took her hand. "You doing okay?"

"Yeah." She smiled. "Just a little sore is all." She met his eye. "Thanks for staying with me. I'm glad you're here."

Damon smiled back. It appeared as if he was about to say something else when the curtain opened and a doctor entered the room.

Eva was manoeuvred to kneel on a chair while the doctor examined her leg. He palpated her calf and she gripped the back of the seat in discomfort. Damon moved closer, rubbing her back. The doctor finished, and let Eva sit again.

The doctor took a seat. "The good news is your Achilles is intact."

Eva sighed with relief.

"The bad news is I think you've torn some muscle fibres. You're going to need physiotherapy."

"Okay." Eva nodded. "That's not too bad."

The doctor smiled. "It does seem that most of the pain is coming from a muscle spasm surrounding the area. So, it should feel better quickly as that calms down. You can self-refer to see the physiotherapist. I can give you the details."

"Thank you," Eva said.

She was given some strong painkillers and took a couple before they left, although the pain was already lessening. *The muscle spasm must be easing*.

She checked the time as she limped from the department with Damon supporting her. *Midday*. They'd only been a couple of hours, so hopefully she hadn't spoiled his afternoon. He helped her into the car and they set off for Eva's parents' house.

When they arrived, he assisted her inside and up the stairs, which were still pretty tricky.

She collapsed onto her bed and looked at him. "You're an absolute lifesaver. The cinema trip tomorrow is on me. I'll even get you some popcorn."

He smiled. "It's no problem. I'm glad I was around to help. Are you sure you'll be up to the movies tomorrow?"

She sat straighter. "Are you kidding? I bloody well deserve an evening out after this debacle."

He laughed. "I'll pick you up so you don't have to drive. Give your leg another day to recover for work. Will you be able to go in?"

She grinned. "Oh yeah. Doctors don't take a day off sick unless they're actually dead."

He laughed. "Well, don't die, because I don't want to be lonely at the movies by myself."

She shook her head. "I won't."

Damon moved to the door and paused. "Do you need a hand getting into the shower?"

Her gaze locked with his and Eva searched his face for signs that he was joking, but found nothing. For a moment she seriously considered saying yes. *But then I'll look a fool when he says he was only kidding.* She shook her head and laughed. "You've already gone above and beyond the call of duty. I'll see you tomorrow—and thanks again."

"Pleasure." He disappeared down the stairs, the front door shutting quietly behind him.

Chapter Eleven

On Sunday, Eva was ready half an hour early for Damon to pick her up, sitting tapping her nails on the counter. This was the most excited she'd been to see him due to the closeness they'd experienced the day before. Her parents were out, so she sat in silence, waiting.

Eventually the doorbell went and there he was. Eva's insides melted. It didn't matter what the man wore, he still looked like a sex god. But this ensemble was particularly appealing. He sported a soft black jumper that clung to the muscles in his arms, accentuating them further. The darkness of his top seemed to bring out his eyes. It was teamed with black jeans that showed off his muscular thighs.

"Ready?" he asked.

Oh yes. "Yep, let's head out."

In the car they chatted about their day. Despite the ease of their conversation, there was a new tension in the air, which was clearly a result of their physical affection the previous day.

Eva glanced at Damon as he drove and cleared her throat. "Have you spoken to Dave lately?"

"Yes, why?" Damon said, grinning. "Have you spoken to Jane lately?" He glanced at her and winked.

"That depends," Eva said, "on what Dave said when you talked to him."

"I cannot possibly reveal any of my source's secrets." Damon mimed drawing a zip across his lips.

Eva leaned over and mimed pulling the zip back again. "Talk, Evans—or you're in for it."

He laughed, watching the road. "What's it worth?"

She shrugged. "What do you want?"

A smile played on his lips. "I'm sure I can think of something."

Eva's breath caught in her throat.

He paused. "Be my date for the school reunion."

Her pulse picked up pace. "Date?"

"Yeah, like a 'friend date'."

Her heart sank. *Not the friend card again*. This guy was the king of mixed signals. She thought for a moment. What did she have to lose? "Fine. Let's go for it. Now tell me what I want to know."

Damon grinned. "Dave fancies Jane."

Eva waited, but he didn't offer anything else. "What? That's it?"

He shrugged as they went through some lights. "What more do you need to know?"

"I need details."

He hesitated. "Dave…*totally* fancies Jane?"

"*Damon*. You totally steered me a bum deal."

He raised his eyebrows. "I'll have you know that my company is not a bum deal."

She shook her head. "I'll be the judge of that."

He pulled up outside the cinema. "Be my guest."

They walked from the car into the building and stood in line for tickets. The film was due to start straight away so they went into the theatre, the lights dimming as they picked their way to the seats. During the trailers they whispered comments and opinions to each other about the up-and-coming films. They laughed easily together, but Eva was very aware of his close, physical presence.

The room darkened further and the main feature started. Eva wasn't sure what the film was about, but Damon had said it was some sort of life drama. Eva preferred comedies nowadays because she'd had enough drama in real life.

Despite not being her usual genre, the film was good, gripping her from the start, and Eva soon lost herself in the plot. She was carried away in a tide of empathy for the characters, two parents struggling with the illness of their child. However, all the while she was aware of the heat of Damon's arm next to hers. Their hands rested on the seat divide between them, nearly touching. Every few minutes Eva would focus her awareness on her hand and wish that he'd touch her again the way he had the day before.

Eventually, about an hour into the film, he slid his hand closer. She held her breath. He lifted it and placed it on top of hers. She turned her hand over and entwined her fingers in his. Neither of them looked at each other or spoke, but they carried on watching the film in silence. Damon rubbed his thumb over hers. Electricity flowed through her arm and coursed through her entire body. She was holding her breath, scared that any movement on her part might make him break contact. She tried to relax but couldn't keep her attention off the sensations he was creating.

What might happen after this? Would he kiss her when he dropped her home? Should *she* kiss *him*? She really wanted to. Maybe she should even suggest going back to his so that they could be alone....

There was a wail from the screen and her attention was drawn back into what was happening in the movie. She understood what the plot of the film was building up to, the death of the child.

Her insides turned to ice and she inhaled sharply. Damon turned towards her but she couldn't tear her eyes from the screen. The scene climaxed as she predicted. She lifted her hand to her face as silent tears streamed down her cheeks.

She tried to block out the voice in her head. *'It will be all right, won't it, Eva? We've caught it in time?'*

Damon's voice cut through the darkness, heavy with concern. "Eva?"

She tried to answer him but couldn't get any words out. She bowed her head into her hand, unable to watch the final few scenes.

Damon squeezed her hand and leaned in. "Do you want to leave?"

Eva shook her head. She needed time to compose herself before the lights came on and everyone in the theatre saw her like this. She breathed deeply, willing the tears to cease. She rubbed the wetness from her cheeks. She could still feel Damon watching her, and as the lights came up with the credits, he let go of her hand and drew her into him.

She mumbled into his jumper. "Don't be nice to me, Damon, or I'll start again."

He stroked her hair. "Want to tell me what's wrong?"

She sniffed. "It was just an emotional film."

He gave her a squeeze. "I've known you for nearly thirty years and I've never seen you cry. I know something is up."

She hesitated for a second. She wanted to tell him, but she couldn't. She needed to keep it all buried, in case it broke her again. "I'm fine. Honestly."

He lifted her chin. "I know you're not ready to talk about it. But I'm ready to listen, whenever you want."

She glanced down, her throat constricted. "Thank you."

They left the movie theatre for the car with her huddled into his side. Once they got there, she was reluctant to let go, so he tightened his arms around her.

Finally she managed to compose herself enough to look him in the eye. "Good job I invested in this heavy-duty mascara or I'd be getting mistaken for a panda and being transported to the nearest zoo right about now."

Damon smiled. She could tell that he wished she'd open up. She knew everyone else felt the same — her parents, Rachel. It wasn't that she didn't want to... She just found it really hard to put it all into words, to break down the sturdy internal wall she'd built to protect herself. She'd always been like that to a degree, but when she'd been a soft, naive junior doctor, the emotional and psychological trauma she'd witnessed and experienced meant she'd had to strengthen her defences. Then Callum's behaviour had solidified it, added armoured guards and its very own moat.

The drive home was silent except for the voice in Eva's head, which was getting louder. *'Please, Eva, don't let this be it. I'll do anything…'*

The tears were close, only a kind word away, and she willed Damon to stay silent.

They pulled into the driveway, and he killed the engine. She daren't look at him, but she reached out and took his hand. He responded with a squeeze.

After a moment she turned her gaze to him. His profile was so handsome. He met her eyes and she willed the words to come. She tried to tell him how much she wanted to confide in him, for him to be the first she'd told the full story to apart from Callum, who hadn't really listened or cared. But she couldn't.

Damon smiled. "I know, Evie. It's okay."

Eva lifted her hand to his cheek. He closed his eyes for a second and moved into her touch.

She finally regained the power of speech, but it was hardly a breakthrough. "Thank you. I'll text you tomorrow." She dropped her hand, opened the car door and walked towards the house.

Chapter Twelve

Damon headed out of the changing room and along the corridor towards the gym. He opened the door and surveyed the room, the whoosh of the air conditioning hitting him in the face. It wasn't busy on a weekday evening and that's how he preferred it. He spotted a free treadmill in his favourite spot next to the glass window overlooking the pool and spa area, climbed on and selected his program. The machine started up and he began to walk faster, adding his ear buds. The high tempo music began, and he picked up the pace.

This was just what he needed to work off the thoughts racing round and round in his mind. Everything with Eva was getting more complicated, and he was sure it was his own fault for having feelings for her that were not just platonic.

When she'd injured her leg, he'd lost the ability to hold back. She'd seemed so unusually vulnerable. At least he hadn't let it go further than a cuddle and some comforting, tactile gestures. But at the cinema the temptation to hold her hand was too intense, and he was sure that if she hadn't become distressed at the film, he wouldn't have been able to resist kissing her.

What was it that'd upset her so much? There was no way it was just the film, as moving as it was. He'd messaged her the next day to say he was there for her whenever she wanted to talk and she'd replied with a heartfelt thank you — but not volunteered anything else.

Something was going on with her and he wished she'd confide in him. The depth to which Damon was desperate for Eva to connect with him as a confidante surprised him. Although they'd known each other forever, they'd hardly seen each other the past few years. Yet pretty much as soon as he'd laid eyes on her at that first meeting, he'd felt the strength of their reconnection. It all just fell into place with Eva — the ease of their playful banter, the laughs they shared, the way he could tell her anything and she'd listen intently and be able to empathise with where he was coming from. He didn't have that with any of his other friends, not to the same degree anyway. That was why he was so desperate not to mess it up.

The one problem he had was he couldn't read how she felt about him. He could tell she liked him as a friend, and he was even pretty sure there was a spark of chemistry, but it seemed she was holding back. He thought it might be because she didn't find him attractive enough to take it further. That was why he'd been trying not to act on impulse. He didn't want to inappropriately read into things and overstep the mark.

Maybe she still saw him as the class clown from school and not someone to be taken seriously. Or perhaps was she still infatuated with Callum. That last one must be a factor, Damon decided. Eva hadn't spelled it out because she was clearly humiliated about it, but the guy must have done the dirty in some way. He was probably the one who had walked away from her and she was yearning for him to take her back. *Shit.* If she was still hung up on that smooth-talking Scotsman, there was no way Damon would be able to convince her to give him a second glance.

The only conclusion was to keep his feelings in lock down so that he didn't frighten her off. But it was difficult. He couldn't help letting the flirty comments slip from his stupid mouth. She was so gorgeous and sexy. Every time he saw her, he had an overwhelming desire to be near her. When he wasn't with her, he was constantly fighting the wanderings of his mind as he imagined peeling off layer after layer of her clothing until he could see just how beautiful she was naked. *For God's sake, it's happening again.* The treadmill wasn't working this time. Maybe if he had a cold shower and a swim in the pool, that might serve him better. He slowed the treadmill to a stop, grabbed his towel, rubbed it over his face and hair and clambered off the machine, the image of what Eva might look like standing before him in her underwear playing on his mind.

* * * *

Eva let the hot shower run over her face. Jane had organised for Eva and Rachel to attend the spa for treatments and for all of them to use the facilities together once she clocked off.

Rachel tipped her head back into the poolside shower next to Eva. "I'm *so* relaxed. That facial was heaven."

"I know," Eva said through the water. "I could just lie down and go to sleep."

Rachel glanced down. "Is your leg okay now?"

"Yeah, much better, thanks," Eva said.

Rachel paused. "By the way, if they don't like you, guys don't drop everything to literally carry you into the hospital then stay with you while you get sorted."

Eva rolled her eyes. "I know he *likes* me. We're friends."

Rachel sighed. "You know what I mean."

She wondered if she should tell Rachel how tactile Damon had been. She might as well, Rachel had already guessed Eva's true feelings anyway.

"What!" Rachel said, so loudly that Eva had to shush her. "He *so* fancies you."

"Rachel," Eva groaned. "Can we *not* talk about it?"

"Why not? This needs to be talked about."

"Because I've messed it all up."

"How?"

Eva hesitated. "I cried at that bloody film. I didn't know what it was about and got emotional. You know, because of Callum."

Rachel didn't say anything.

Eva cleared her throat. "So, you know, he saw me all upset and will've known it was about Callum so it will've put him off. Plus I'm really ugly when I cry."

"Okay…" Rachel said. "Are you sure that was the only reason you were upset? What was the movie about?

"Nothing major," Eva said quickly. "Just relationship problems."

Rachel hesitated. Her voice was quiet. "Do you think you were emotional because of Oliver?"

Ice stabbed into Eva's gut at the mention of that name. "No. And I don't want to talk about him."

"Okay," Rachel said gently. "Listen… I'm sure it's retrievable. Don't worry."

Eva swallowed down her racing heart, forcing Oliver's name and all thoughts of him into the dark recess of her mind. It was good that Rachel didn't know the whole story.

Jane joined them and they headed for the Jacuzzi, climbing in. The water was so warm and comforting. Eva felt as if she might lay her head on the pile of bubbles frothing next to her and float off to sleep.

Rachel's voice cut through the sleep cloud in Eva's mind. "What was the lowdown from Damon about Dave?"

Eva sat straighter to wake herself up. "His exact words were 'Dave fancies Jane'. No, wait, 'Dave *totally* fancies Jane.'"

Jane's cheeks flushed and Eva suspected that was not a result of the heat from the Jacuzzi.

Rachel leaned back into the froth. "Excellent. Now we need to get planning for the reunion. It's not long away."

Jane frowned. "Planning, as in what?"

Rachel held up her hand. "Don't panic. I just mean we need to make sure you two have drop dead gorgeously sexy outfits and sort out tactics."

Eva looked at her. "The two of us? But it's only Jane we're trying to fix up."

Rachel laughed. "Yeah right. We're also on 'mission Damon' here, you know."

Eva rolled her eyes. "It's a lost cause. Just call it a day, will you?"

Rachel shook her head. "Never."

Eva shrank farther into the bubbles.

Rachel went on about how they would all meet at the bar for a drink then walk along to the hotel for the reunion.

Eva didn't want to think about it anymore. "Okay whatever you want. I'm going for a swim. It's too hot in here and I'm about to fall asleep."

Eva climbed out of the Jacuzzi and walked the short distance to the swimming pool. It was empty and the blue water shimmered invitingly. She lowered herself in and a shock of cold jolted through her. She quickly pushed herself off and swam, trying to warm up.

She moved her limbs in a breaststroke to take her to the other end of the pool and back again. Rachel and Jane were crossing along the side from the Jacuzzi to the steam room, and she gave them a wave. She contacted the side and pushed off again. The water rippled over her, soothing her muscles.

After a number of lengths, she touched the side and held on for a moment. Eyeing the hydrotherapy pool on the right, she placed her palms on the edge and pushed herself up and out. She ran a hand over her wet hair and stepped forward, about to turn and walk on towards the hydrotherapy area, when she discovered that Damon was in the gym on the other side of the glass partition.

Eva froze. He was climbing off a treadmill, glowing with perspiration and the muscles in his arms and legs appearing even more pumped up than usual. He caught her gaze as he rubbed a towel over his face and appeared shocked for a second.

She was rooted to the spot, taken off-guard at the fact he was there and unprepared for the onslaught of heat inside her, spreading like wildfire through every nerve-ending in her body. She willed herself to do something but she couldn't move. He lifted his hand in a wave then gestured that he was coming through to the pool. She managed a half-wave half-thumbs up gesture and walked away into the hydrotherapy area.

Shit. He was coming in there any minute and she'd made a fool of herself. There's no way he wouldn't have noticed that she was practically drooling over him through that glass. With a start she realised that he'd be wearing even less clothing. How was she going to contain herself then? She looked around for Rachel and Jane to come rescue her, but they'd left the steam room for the sauna only minutes before and weren't showing any signs of reappearing.

She climbed into the hydrotherapy pool, which was cooler than the Jacuzzi but also bubbling away and watched the door of the men's changing room, torn between wanting to see Damon and the urge to run off and hide. He wasn't there. Had he changed his mind and gone home?

Then he appeared. Eva sucked in her breath. His hair and skin were wet and glistening from the shower he'd clearly taken post-gym, small beads of water clinging to his muscular form. He was wearing navy swim shorts that came to mid-thigh. She took in the contours of those fit thighs and calves, his toned chest and abdomen.

Eva willed herself to stop staring at his body before he glanced up and caught her — and only just managed it. He gave her a wave and walked over. After he broke eye contact to start walking, she raked her gaze over his body again. The fire burning inside her threatened to consume her and she was relieved to be sitting in cool water.

Damon lowered himself into the pool and moved towards her. *Oh my God, he's so sexy.*

Damon sat on one of the underwater shelves across from her. "Hello. Wasn't expecting to see you here."

Eva willed her voice to appear. "Rachel and I met Jane here after work for some treatments. They're just cooking themselves in the sauna over there."

He smiled. "Didn't you want to go in?"

"Nah, I can't take the heat." She caught his gaze, the heat in her own face rising by about ten degrees. She swallowed. "Are you a member of the gym?"

He nodded. "I usually come in the evening after work because it's easier to get on the equipment. The pool's really nice after a workout too."

He sank farther into the water and rested his elbows onto the sides behind him. Eva studied the muscles in his arms. Where were Rachel and Jane when she needed them?

She cleared her throat. "What're you doing at the weekend?"

He looked her in the eye again and she thought she was going to melt and become one with the pool. "On Friday I said I'd meet Dave for a drink in the Swan, and I was thinking…" He shifted across to come sit next to her. "After what we were discussing about Dave and Jane, I wondered if you two would want to join us on Friday? It might break the ice a bit for them to have a drink together before the reunion."

Eva used all her willpower to drag her thoughts away from the fact that his practically naked body was right next her while she weighed up the idea.

"That's sounds good. I'll run it past Jane and hopefully she'll go for it."

He smiled. "Great. We'll get these two kids together yet. We're just like our mums."

Eva laughed. "I hope not."

He was so close. She thought his arm brushed against hers through the bubbles of the pool. For a moment he flicked his gaze to her mouth, then the door of the steam room hoisted open and he turned his head towards it. Rachel and Jane came out onto the poolside, looking flushed.

Damon turned back to Eva. "I'm going to jump in the pool. Let me know what Jane reckons about Friday."

She nodded. "Okay, thanks."

He stood and climbed out of the water. As he walked along to the main pool, he stopped and exchanged a greeting and a brief chat with her friends, who appeared surprised to see him. Then he lowered himself into the main pool and start swimming lengths. He used a front crawl and Eva admired the form of his arms and legs as he cut through the water.

"Ahem."

Eva startled, realizing that Rachel and Jane were now in the pool next to her but she'd been oblivious to their arrival.

"What?" Eva asked.

Rachel smiled. "What're you staring at?"

"Nothing," Eva said, moving her hands through the water. "Just thinking how nice this pool is."

"And how nice the view is," Rachel muttered under her breath.

Jane smiled and gave Eva a sympathetic look. "What're you guys doing at the weekend?"

Rachel leaned back. "We've got Marcus' family coming to visit."

Eva glanced up. "Jane and I are going to the pub on Friday night."

Jane frowned. "We are?"

Eva nodded. "Damon was just telling me he and Dave are going, and he asked us along as well."

Rachel's eyes lit up. "Perfect. A double date."

"It's not a *date*," Eva said quickly, spotting the expression of terror on Jane's face. "Just four friends having a drink."

"Okay, whatever you want to call it." Rachel rubbed her hands together. "It still means my plan is coming together."

Eva looked at Rachel with raised eyebrows. Then she turned to Jane. "Is that okay? I've not committed to it yet, so if you don't want to then that's no problem."

Jane smiled. "Yes. I'll be a bit nervous, but I think it'll be a good laugh."

Eva watched Damon get out of the pool and give them a wave as he headed into the changing room. She smiled. "I think so too."

Chapter Thirteen

Eva put on a strappy top paired with her jeans and went downstairs to find her jacket and boots. She chose a soft faux leather grey jacket and her short wedge boots. As soon as she finished pulling on the last one, the doorbell went and there was Jane, looking lovely but terrified. Jane lived a bit farther away, but she'd been keen to call for Eva to walk to the pub together because she didn't want to arrive on her own. The guys were going to be there already, because they were meeting straight from work.

Eva left the house. "Jane, don't look so scared."

Jane blew out a deep breath. "Sorry. I feel sick."

Eva hugged her then left her arm around her shoulders as they started to walk along the road. "Don't worry. It's just a little drink, and all four of us will be there together. You can just have a casual chat with Dave and see how it goes."

Jane took a breath in and out again. "You're right. I need to calm down. I'm just making this into something bigger than it is because I really like Dave and, before this, I've been in the same relationship since school."

Eva dropped her arm and gave Jane a nudge. "And he really likes you too, don't forget."

Jane nodded, though she still appeared unconvinced.

They arrived at the pub. As they made their way through the periphery of people towards the bar, Eva scouted around for Damon and Dave. She spotted them at a table nearby.

They headed over. Dave saw them first and stood, meeting them halfway to the table.

He greeted Eva first with a kiss on the cheek. "Hey, Eva, long time, no see." He leaned into her ear. "Thanks for coming."

Eva smiled. "Great to see you."

Dave turned to Jane and they gave each other a hug.

Over Dave's shoulder, Damon was getting up.

Dave smiled. "What can I get you to drink?

"G and T please," said Eva.

Jane nodded. "The same for me, thank you."

Dave went to the bar and Eva walked over to Damon. He enveloped her in a tight hug. It took her off guard because she'd sensed he'd been holding back on the friendly affection since the cinema incident. He let her go and gave Jane a peck on the cheek before the three of them sat, Eva next to Damon and across from Jane.

Eva touched his arm. "You all right? What time did you guys get here?"

He rubbed his face. "About five-thirty. And no, not really. Bloody Dave drinks like a fish and he's been getting the beers in like there's no tomorrow. It's gone to my head, especially because I've not had anything to eat since lunchtime."

Eva studied Damon's face. His eyes did seem a little glazed.

Jane smiled. "Did you ask Dave to get you a soft drink this round?"

Damon nodded. "Yeah, but just wait and see what he comes back with."

Dave approached the table with a tray of drinks. "Right, gin and tonic for Eva, the same for Jane and a pint of lager for Damon."

Damon rolled his eyes.

Eva laughed. "Not sure that was Damon's exact order, Dave."

Dave shrugged, smiling. "I've no idea what you mean."

He sat next to Jane and started chatting easily to her.

Damon leaned over to Eva's ear. "Dave was keen for some Dutch courage, hence the early start."

Eva shivered. Damon's lips had lightly brushed her ear as he spoke. She nodded and turned her head to whisper back to him. "Jane's really nervous, but it looks like he's putting her at ease. 'Mission matchmaker' is a go."

Damon smiled, then leaned back in. "All this beer has taken its toll. I need to visit the facilities. Keep an eye on our little love birds for me while I'm gone."

"No worries, Cupid." Eva mimed shooting a bow and arrow.

Damon stood and headed towards the rest rooms, swaying slightly as he went.

She turned back to the others. "I think Damon's struggling." She smiled. "Is he a bit of a lightweight nowadays?"

Dave rolled his eyes. "Oh yeah, absolutely. He's been on this health kick since things went south for him and Sarah — at the gym loads and hardly drinking any alcohol." He smiled, his tone affectionate. "Freak."

"Ah, okay," Eva said. "We might be carrying him home at this rate."

Dave grinned. "Wouldn't be the first time, Eva." He started telling them a few tales of alcohol-related shenanigans that he and Damon had been involved in in the past.

They were all laughing as Damon approached the table.

He took his seat next to Eva. "What's so funny?"

Dave tapped the side of his nose. "Just giving the ladies some important background info on you."

Damon raised his eyebrows. "That sounds dubious."

Eva laughed. "I never knew that the traffic cone on top of the statue in town was your doing."

Damon shook his head. "Trust Dave to be giving away all my secrets."

The four of them chatted about school days and traded funny stories. Eva had everyone in stitches with some tales from when she worked in A&E. "So the guy reckoned he'd fallen on it," she concluded. "And that's how it got lodged up there."

"*Fell* on it?" Dave said. "How do you *fall* onto a cucumber?"

Eva laughed. "It's a common excuse when it comes to objects stuck in orifices."

Jane was wiping tears from her eyes.

Dave shook his head. "You've got the best stories. You should be an after-dinner speaker."

Eva smiled. "I'm not sure these are the sorts of tales that go with dinner."

She glanced at Damon. A few more drinks in and he seemed decidedly worse for wear. Eva had already been to the bar to get packets of crisps for him in order to soak up some of the alcohol, but it hadn't helped much. She watched Dave and Jane, who were talking intimately, and wondered what to do. Damon needed to go home now. He was in no fit state to go alone and she doubted a taxi would take him. But she didn't want Dave to be the one to accompany him, because he and Jane were getting on so well.

She made the decision, and signalled to the others. "Guys, I'm going to get Damon home. I think he needs a lie down."

They looked over at him. He had his elbow on the table and his head resting in his hand.

Dave drained his drink. "I'll take him. You and Jane stay on for another one."

Eva studied Jane. There was disappointment in her eyes. Eva shook her head. "You stay with Jane. I'll take him. Make sure she gets home safe, though, or you're in for it."

He laughed and saluted her. "Absolutely, you can count on me."

"Is that okay?" Eva asked Jane.

Jane smiled broadly. "Of course it is. Text me to let me know you get back safe." It was clear that Jane was more than happy to be left in Dave's company.

Eva nodded. "The same goes for you. Message me once you get home." She stood. "Right. Come on, Evans. Bedtime for you." She pulled Damon's arm round her shoulder, lifting him from the chair.

Damon could walk, but he was unsteady. "Where're we going?" he asked as she helped him out of the pub and onto the street.

"I'm taking you home. You need to sleep this off."

He sighed. "Okay. As long as you don't try to take advantage of me in my vulnerable state."

"Don't worry. You're in safe hands. Trust me. I'm a doctor."

Luckily the walk to Damon's wasn't far. It only took fifteen minutes normally. However, the pace was a little slower on this occasion because Damon kept stopping to narrate various random points of interest and Eva would have to coax him along again.

When they eventually arrived at his front door, Eva asked him for his keys. He patted the pockets of his jeans and gave her a horrified look.

Eva sighed. "Don't tell me you've lost your keys or you'll feel the wrath of Mathers."

He grinned. "Just joking. They're in my pocket." He fumbled around for a minute. "Fiddly bloody keys...."

Eva shook her head. "Right... Let me get them." She stuck her hand in his pocket, grasped the keys, pulled them out and started unlocking the front door.

He raised his hands. "Hey, no manhandling. You promised."

She helped him through the door. "Sorry... Needs must." It seemed as if he'd gotten more drunk on the journey home. That last drink must've still been making its way into his system.

Eva positioned herself behind Damon in order to usher him upstairs. "Okay, straight up. You need to lie down before you fall down."

She went after him to ensure that he didn't topple backward. Once they reached the landing, she steadied him into his bedroom and he sat heavily on the bed. He was still swaying from side to side, even when sitting.

She placed her hands on his shoulders. "Do you just want to sleep in your clothes? It'll be easier," she said.

He shook his head in an exaggerated manner. "It's not comfy."

She scanned the room. "Where're your PJs?"

He shut his eyes. "I don't wear them. I sleep in my underwear."

Eva groaned inwardly. She was going to have to help strip him down. That was going to be torture.

He lifted his hands and fiddled with the buttons on his shirt. "It's okay, though. I can manage." He couldn't even catch hold of the individual buttons.

Eva batted his hands away and knelt to help. "Come here."

She undid each button carefully, trying not to touch his bare skin for fear that she may explode into a flaming ball of lust.

Then she took the shirt off, keeping her eyes away from his torso. "You need to stand now." She lifted him to his feet, and quickly got his jeans belt and button undone before he could collapse onto the bed. She had only just gotten the jeans down when he did just that, sitting heavily.

"I haven't got the duvet back yet. You need to stand again."

He shook his head. "I can't."

Eva knelt in front of him. "Why not? I'll help you."

He cupped her face. "You're so beautiful."

Eva thought her heart might explode. "Damon—"

"No, listen. You really are beautiful. I'm not just saying that cause I'm drunk," he said, slurring his words. "It's true. You're my best friend, Evie. My BF. My BFF. Wait! How many Fs are there?"

"Come on," she said gently. "Let me get you under the covers."

But he just drew her face nearer to his. He was still gorgeous, even when he was pissed.

He smiled. "Thanks for looking after me."

He leaned forward and gently kissed her lips, like he meant to give her a small peck then draw away again. But as soon as he made contact, he lingered on, moving his lips slowly over hers, tasting her softly. It was the most gentle of butterfly kisses but fire still burned deep in her belly. She kissed him back for a couple of seconds then came to her senses and broke contact. She didn't want this to happen when he was so drunk. It wasn't fair to him — to either of them. As she moved away, he collapsed onto the pillow.

"Damon?"

He was out for the count.

Reeling with shock at what'd just happened, she went onto autopilot, pulling the duvet from under him, lifting his legs into bed and covering him up. Then she went downstairs and fetched him a glass of water to go on his bedside table. She watched him for a moment, then went into the en suite and brought the bin into the bedroom, placing it by the bed in case he'd be sick in the night.

That anxiety started building, so she took a pillow and placed it behind him to try to keep him on his side. If he vomited lying on his back, he might choke. Again, she stood to survey the situation. Would that be enough? He might still be able to roll over. He was practically unconscious now, so if he did vomit choking would be a real hazard.

Eva wondered if she should sleep on the sofa downstairs to keep an eye on him. But she knew that would be pointless because there'd be no way she'd hear him from down there if he were in trouble.

She groaned. She was going to have to sleep next to him to keep watch. If he started to vomit, the noise would wake her and she'd be able to make sure he stayed on his side or sat up.

This truly was torture. She'd be lying right next to the man of her dreams and he'd be naked except for a pair of tight boxers. There was no way she'd get a wink of sleep.

Eva looked around the room and spotted a T-shirt and a pair of cotton shorts. She glanced at Damon. He was still out cold, so she quickly stripped to her underwear and put on the T-shirt and shorts. Then she turned off the light and slid into bed next to him, painstakingly making sure she didn't make contact with him.

She lay there for ages, mind and heart in competition to outrace each other. What was the deal with that kiss? What did it mean?

Eventually the relatively small amount of alcohol she had ingested took its toll and she closed her eyes, drifting off to sleep.

A couple of hours later she awoke with a start. Damon was making noises that indicated he was about to vomit. She leapt out of bed and around the other side, grabbed the bin and placed it under his face, holding the back of his head so he couldn't roll over. After he'd finished, she wiped his face carefully with some tissues and disposed of the bin contents into the toilet, cleaning it afterwards. Then after returning the bin to its post, she slid back into the bed. Even clearing up after him in this situation didn't make her find him any less attractive. *That's a bad sign.* Eventually she fell back to sleep.

* * * *

Damon woke up. The room was bathed in sunlight and it hurt his eyes. Why were his surroundings moving as if he were at sea? He blinked. *Where am I?* He waited for the spinning to slow and recognized his bedroom. Why did it feel like he'd been stabbed through the head and the contents of the Sahara Desert emptied into his mouth? *What happened last night?* He shut his eyes and tried to remember. He'd met Dave in the pub. They'd had some drinks, some more drinks, then Eva and Jane had arrived and yet more drinks. There was a pattern emerging here. *Bloody Dave.* Then what?

Crap. Eva had had to walk him home. He screwed his eyes tight shut. Then she'd helped him into his own house and upstairs to the bedroom. His head throbbed. *Oh no.* She ended up having to help him undress and get into bed.

He groaned, and something shifted in the bed behind him. *Holy shit.* He painstakingly rolled onto his back to glance over the bed. Eva was there, sleeping peacefully. She was wearing his T-shirt and she looked fantastic. *No.* He hadn't had sex with her, had he? This was *so* not the way he'd imagined it happening.

Think. He was positive that after she'd helped him undress that he'd passed out. Things were at their haziest at that point in his memory, but there was no way he would've been physically capable of sex at that point. In any case, Eva wouldn't have been interested.

He let himself relax and lay there watching her sleep, thinking how much he wanted to kiss her right now and trying not to think how much of a fool he'd made of himself. He'd need to apologize to her as soon as she awoke. At that point, her eyelids fluttered and she peered at him from under them.

Her voice was thick with sleep. "Morning, you old drunkard."

His throat was dry. "Hi. I'm so sorry."

She blinked. "What for?"

He tried to lubricate his mouth. "For getting drunk and acting like an idiot. I'm sorry for it all," he said quickly, trying to make amends. "I wish none of it had happened."

Eva frowned. "None of it?"

He tried to nod but it made the pounding in his head worse. "Of course. It was a complete lapse of judgment and there's no way it'll be happening again."

She was quiet for a moment then she smiled brightly. "No problem. Let's forget it happened. Oh, just to explain, I stayed with you because I was worried you might vomit in the night and choke to death — not because I was trying to take advantage of you." She sat up. "A pesky side effect of being a doctor is the paranoia."

Damon spotted a glass of water on his bedside table and took a sip. "Thanks. You're a star." He took another drink. "I wasn't actually sick, though, was I?"

Eva shrugged. "Only a little."

Damon covered his face with his hands. "Oh God, this is so embarrassing."

Eva laughed gently, clearly attuned to the fact that he couldn't stand any loud noises. "It's okay. We both have dirt on the other now. It only makes the bond of friendship stronger." She got out of bed. "I'll freshen up then I'd better head home or Mum'll get the wrong idea."

"Okay," he said, watching her go into the en suite. He closed his eyes, sleep drifting close by. The floorboards creaked. He awoke to Eva standing by the bedroom door.

"Sorry," she said. "I was trying to sneak out and not wake you. I left you some painkillers by your glass of water. Can I get you anything else?"

This time he was sensible enough not to shake his head. "No, that's okay. You've done more than your duty. I really am grateful, even though I'm totally embarrassed."

She smiled. "Forget it. It's fine." She waved her hand in front of her face as if performing magic. "None of this ever happened."

Damon managed to lean on one elbow. "I hope two weeks is long enough to get rid of my hangover and be ready for the reunion."

Eva laughed. "You'd better not let Dave get the drinks that night."

Damon managed a small laugh, although then he had to hold his forehead because it throbbed painfully.

Eva opened the door. "I'll text you about the reunion."

"Okay. See you soon," Damon said, as she closed the door quietly. He lay back carefully for the sake of his head, took the painkillers and closed his eyes. Thank goodness he'd managed to salvage that situation, and all was well.

Chapter Fourteen

Eva trudged along Damon's street, feeling like she was treading on her own heart with each step.

'I'm sorry for it all. I wish none of it had happened... It was a complete lapse of judgment and there's no way it'll be happening again.'

Remembering his words was like a knife to her gut. He thought kissing her was a mistake and he wished he could take it back.

When was she going to learn? Every time she thought he might feel more for her than just friendship, she ended up feeling like this. She needed to stop before she got really hurt, although it already pained her pretty badly.

She wished he'd stop giving her false hope. As much as she enjoyed the flirty comments and affection, it really wasn't doing her any good. If things were the same at the reunion, she'd have to tell him to lay off.

Time counted down to the day of the reunion. Rachel had gone into planning overdrive and arranged where the six of them would meet. Eva hadn't the heart to tell Rachel about Damon kissing her then saying it was a mistake, so her friends were still labouring under the misapprehension that something might happen between them.

Eva met up with Rachel, Marcus and Jane at a bar near the hotel where the reunion would take place. They got there an hour or so before Damon and Dave were due to arrive because Rachel said she wanted to buy Eva and Jane a round of champagne to celebrate her partnership, though Eva suspected Rachel's ulterior motive was to provide Eva with some Dutch courage prior to Damon's arrival.

Once the bottle was drained, Eva made her way to the bar to get the next round. She adjusted her little black dress, one of the purchases from her shopping trip with Meena. A breeze brushed against her back, the rear of the dress was open from the neck to the small of her back with black strands of material connecting the gap. She turned her head to look at the source of the breeze, the open doorway. Damon was stood there. She willed her heart to slow as she watched him survey the room. His eyes locked onto hers and his expression darkened for a moment.

Eva steadied herself as the onslaught of longing washed over her. She took a deep breath and gave him a wave.

The barman asked for her order and with a sterling effort, she wrenched her gaze away from Damon. When she turned back, he and Dave were at their table greeting the others, but Damon kept glancing at her. She signalled him to come over, indicating she wanted to know what drinks they wanted.

When he reached her he gave her a hug. "You look gorgeous."

She hugged him back, her head swimming with his scent. "Thank you." *Remember not to read anything into his compliments.* "What're you guys drinking?"

He smiled. "A bottle of beer for me please—and a pint for Dave."

She turned to the barman to add the two extras onto her previous request.

Damon helped her carry the drinks over to the table and they handed them out. Eva passed him his bottle and her fingers brushed his.

He smiled. "Thank you."

She gave him a healthy dose of eye contact. "No problem." The champagne had indeed made her a little bolder. She was starting to think that two could play at his little flirting game.

The hotel was only a short distance away and eventually they headed out of the bar to walk to the reunion. By this time, the party should be in full swing.

Eva found herself at the back of the group with Damon, so she decided to embrace her newly found boldness. He was always meaninglessly flirting, so now it was her turn.

She put her arm through his and pretended that she couldn't feel the butterflies fluttering in her stomach or the heat that shocked through her every time she looked at him. He, somewhat annoyingly, seemed very at ease with it.

She squeezed his arm. "By the way, I should probably warn you that I heard Tracey McKenna is going to be on the prowl for you tonight."

He frowned. "What?"

"Yep," Eva said. "Apparently she wants to rekindle the old chemistry." She leaned in and nodded towards Dave, who was in front, walking hand in hand with Jane. "I can be your wingman if you'd like, seeing as Dave will be out of commission."

Damon raised his eyebrows. "Old chemistry? Don't tell me you heard about that."

She shrugged. "We were sixteen years old and she dragged you into a bush in the park one evening. *Everyone* heard about it. In fact it was all our entire class year talked about for two whole weeks."

Eva remembered every detail of the rumour that had gone round their year about Damon and Tracey — the boy she loved and the girl who made her feel about two inches tall getting together. It had broken her heart at the time.

Damon cursed under his breath. "I can assure you that I'm not the slightest bit interested in Tracey McKenna."

Eva winked at him. "Whatever you say."

He gave her a slow smile. "I mean it, Eva. Tracey is not the one I'm interested in."

"Okay…" Eva said, the intonation in her voice rising at the end as if she were questioning him.

"Watch it, Mathers," Damon told her, pulling his elbow to his side so that she was drawn into him. "Any more of your cheek and I'll have to bend you over my knee."

Eva shrugged. "Promises, promises." She smiled and kept her gaze straight ahead, then stole a sideways glance at him.

He was watching her with a grin on his face.

She looked ahead again.

Damon laughed. "I might need to employ you as my bodyguard rather than wingman. I'd better not drink too much again in case she attacks me. Hey, did you notice I've been sticking to bottles of beer tonight rather than pints?" He winked at her in an exaggerated manner. "Tactics."

She laughed. "Good choice. Don't want you passing out again."

He cocked his head to one side. "Although if that *were* to happen, I would of course have my personal physician to tend to me."

She nodded. "True. Though I'm not sure you can afford my private fees."

He raised his eyebrows. "How much would I owe?"

She shrugged, enjoying her newfound role as an insufferable flirt. *Lydia Bennett, eat your heart out.* "Let's see what we can work out."

She felt his eyes on her. "You look beautiful."

Despite her best efforts, her heart did a somersault. *No. Don't fall for it this time. Don't let yourself hope.*

She turned and met his gaze. "Thank you. You're very handsome yourself. Blue suits you."

He was wearing a light blue shirt and dark trousers and was indeed very handsome. But then again, she thought he looked handsome in anything.

Damon smiled. It appeared as if he was about to say something, but just then they arrived at the front door of the hotel. Everyone was going inside.

He took her hand to help her up the steps. She went ahead of him and joined Rachel and Jane in the reception area.

Rachel gestured along the hallway. "It's in the suite down there." The six of them followed the corridor into a huge room.

"Wow," Jane said. "They've done a great job."

Eva nodded, taking in the large welcome banner. There were big round tables around the periphery of the room, which had all been decorated with fresh flowers. There were also copies of the class photos from their year placed in photo holders.

Their group headed to an empty table to deposit their jackets. The DJ was playing at the front just under the banner and next to a huge dance floor, which was already pretty packed. There was a bar at the back with a long buffet table running along the wall adjacent to it.

Damon came to stand next to Eva. "What can I get you guys to drink?"

He placed his hand on the small of Eva's back and she tried to suppress the resulting shudder of desire. It was difficult because the partially open nature at the rear meant that his fingers were touching her bare skin.

Jane and Rachel requested their drinks and Damon turned to Eva. He stroked his thumb lightly across her skin and her head spun.

"I'll have the same as Rach, please." She had no idea what she'd just ordered because she'd been so distracted by his touch. He smiled and dropped his hand to move to the bar.

Rachel huddled the girls together. "Right, I want an update. Jane, how's it going with Dave?"

Jane smiled broadly. "Great. We haven't kissed yet but I'm really hoping it'll happen tonight."

Eva touched Jane's arm. "I'm so pleased it's going well. Dave's a great guy."

Jane glanced at the floor, still smiling. "He is, isn't he?"

"You guys are so lovely together," Rachel said. "I'm sure you'll be smooching away before the night is out."

Jane looked at Eva. "What about you and Damon?"

Eva frowned. "It's complicated."

"It doesn't need to be. Just go for it." Rachel said.

Eva raised her eyebrows. "I'll handle it my own way."

Rachel held her hands up. "Okay, handle away." She craned her neck towards the bar. "Where're our drinks? Oh, there's Marcus now."

Marcus approached and handed each of them a glass, then was taken to one side by someone who recognized him. Eva tried to spot Damon but couldn't.

A female voice called out from behind her. "Hi!"

Eva closed her eyes for a second, her heart rate picking up. "Hi, Tracey."

Tracey drew up next to Eva. She was wearing the tallest stilettos Eva had ever seen and she found herself trying not to speak to Tracey's chest, which was nearly at eye level and peering out of her strapless dress at her.

"Well," Tracey said, looking Eva up and down. "Don't you look...*cute.*"

Rachel rolled her eyes. "I think you pronounced 'drop dead gorgeous' incorrectly."

Tracey hesitated, clearly thrown off her stride. "Yeah...that's what I meant."

Rachel raised her eyebrows. "Then say what you mean."

Tracey tossed her hair over her shoulder. "You'd better get that drink in you, Rachel. It might sweeten you temper. Anyone seen Damon?"

Eva shook her head. "Not for a while."

Tracey glanced around the room. "Okay. I'll see you later." She turned and walked towards the bar.

"Good riddance," muttered Rachel.

Eva touched her arm and smiled. She was grateful for Rachel sticking up for her, even if she was rather blunt about it. "Thanks, Rach."

Rachel circled her shoulders and gave her a squeeze.

Jane shook her head. "She's so mean."

"You're not wrong," Rachel said. "The woman's a bully. She used to be horrible to us all at school and now we're just supposed to forget about it? Why do some women seem to think that tearing the rest of us down will elevate their own self esteem?"

Eva sighed. "I figured that everyone had changed and grown up—but maybe not."

Jane frowned. "I didn't really know her at school. I'm glad now that I didn't."

Rachel nodded. "She was off with Eva in particular, doing her down behind her back and calling her a boring nerd when she got a good grade."

Jane shook her head, frowning. "She must've been jealous of you, Eva."

Eva was starting to think that her initial instinct about coming here was correct. She hadn't fitted in at school and she didn't fit in here.

Respite came in the form of another classmate who approached and greeted them. She took them to join her group of friends and they studied the photos that were being passed around from the nearest table. Eva glanced up to look for Damon. Marcus was laughing with Dave and a couple of others, but Damon wasn't there. She went back to the conversation with her old classmates. Someone had fetched another round of drinks and the alcohol and conversation were both flowing. Eva was surprised to find she was enjoying herself. It occurred to her that high school had been a difficult time for everyone and she was likely not the only one who'd felt out of place and marginalised.

The people they were speaking to drifted in and out, with new people joining for a chat and others heading off for the dance floor. Eva hadn't had chance to get anything from the buffet but she didn't mind because she was having fun. She laughed at something Rachel said and glanced up. She thought she'd spotted Damon across the room and so craned her neck to peer through the crowd.

Eva's insides turned to ice. Tracey McKenna was hanging off him, her arms around his neck as she smiled at him with her scarlet red lips.

A wave of nausea enveloped her. She couldn't see Damon's face, but she imagined him smiling and making one of his flirtatious comments. She drew her mouth into a thin line. She could sense Jane and Rachel looking at her.

"Eva—" Jane said.

Eva shook her head and drained her drink. "I'm going to get some fresh air."

She headed for the door then decided she'd rather have more alcohol. After getting another drink, she surveyed the room. The dance floor was packed, and in the same corner she could see Tracey was still hanging off Damon, her head tipped back as she laughed. Eva gritted her teeth. She headed to the opposite end of the room where she recognized one of her friends from class. She heard from him now and again on social media.

"Hi, Andy," she said as she reached his group.

"Hi," he said. "Great to see you." He turned to his wife who was standing next to him. "Sweetheart, this is Eva. Eva, this is my lovely wife, Nicola."

Eva shook Nicola's hand. How sweet that Andy had specifically added the 'lovely' to describe his wife. He'd always been a great guy. How come she wasn't with a great guy? First Callum had jilted her and now Damon was giving her the run-around. Though when she thought about it, Damon had given her the run-around long before she'd met Callum. She'd been in love with him at school and he hadn't even known she existed. Then he'd gone on to shag Tracey, who'd been a total bitch to her.

A lot of what she was feeling was exaggerated by alcohol but that was little comfort.

Eva became involved in conversation with the new group, which included a couple of single guys. She got the feeling they were staring at her appreciatively in a not-very-subtle manner due to the freely flowing drink—but she didn't care. Someone might as well look at her like that and the phrase 'beggars can't be choosers' entered her mind.

A couple of people drifted away from the group and one of these single guys was then standing next to her.

It was only then that she recognized him—Eric Donovan.

She remembered the echo of Eric and his friends laughing at her and a feeling of humiliation washed over her as acutely and painfully as if it had happened yesterday. Then Damon's voice appeared in her head. *'You mean you haven't heard of Eric Donovan…serial father?'* Eva shuddered at the thought. Eric hadn't been much of a catch because he was a smug git who thought he was God's gift, despite not even being that attractive.

Eric eyed her and grinned. "Hello, Eva. You're looking sexy this evening."

Eva blocked the urge to gag. "Hi, Eric. How're the kids?"

Her dry tone was lost on him. He winked at her. "Oh, fine. Always on the lookout to make some more though."

Eva felt she might vomit, and it wasn't due to the alcohol. She was now on her own with Eric. *Oh hell no.* She was not having this. The evening was getting shitty pretty quickly, so she'd be damned if this smarmy idiot, who'd made her feel like crap at school just for being intelligent, was going to think he could try it on with her.

Eric leaned in, clearly about to use another one of his crappy pick-up lines. She was getting ready to let rip with the mother of all knock backs when an arm slid around her waist from the opposite side and a male form leaned in front of her, effectively blocking Eric's advance. Eva smelled Damon's scent before she spotted him.

He spoke at her ear loud enough for Eric to hear. "There you are, gorgeous. I've been looking for you." Damon leaned back and met her gaze. She could tell exactly what he was up to.

Damon addressed Eric without looking at him, a dangerous edge to his voice. "Eric, excuse us."

Eric nodded, muttering "no problem," but appearing as if it was in fact a really big one.

Damon led Eva away towards the door where it was less crowded. She opened her mouth to say something, but he drew her into him, his lips grazing her ear. "Just a minute... He's still watching us." He nuzzled his face into her neck.

Liquid fire spread through her veins. His lips were brushing her skin and every part of her was tingling in response, but she fought it because she was livid. She was sick of this — on the one hand desperate for his affection and grasping at any flirty comment but then disappointed every time he qualified their relationship as platonic. Then, to top it off he'd been all over Tracey bloody McKenna. *Not interested in her, my arse.*

She stayed silent as her rage built.

Damon lifted his head to make eye contact. "Okay, he's slunk off now. I hate to tell you this, but he was only interested in you for your amazing body."

He gave her a look that set her on fire, but it only caused her fury to build further — at him for leading her on again and at herself for being so affected by him. She'd had enough. It was her turn to lead *him* on.

She met his gaze. "How do you know I have an amazing body? You've not seen it. *Yet.*"

His eyes burned into hers and he took a sharp breath.

She stepped away. "Excuse me." She stalked off and disappeared into the throng.

Eva emerged out of the other side and approached their table. Rachel was on Marcus's knee whispering in his ear, clearly taking advantage of a childfree evening. Jane and Dave were a couple of seats along, kissing. Eva's heart swelled, before remembering how angry she was with Damon and crashing fury followed. She reached the table and grabbed her handbag from the chair next to Rachel and Marcus.

"Where've you been?" Rachel said. "We were looking for you. "

Eva turned to go. "Never mind. I'm leaving now. I've well and truly had my fill."

Rachel stood. "Wait a minute."

Marcus frowned. "What's wrong?"

"I'm fine," Eva said. "I've just had enough, so I'm going home."

"We'll walk you," Marcus said.

Rachel nodded, moving towards her coat.

Eva held her hand up. "I want to be on my own. Say bye to Jane and Dave for me. I don't think they're coming up for air anytime soon." She turned and started to walk away.

"Okay, but text when you get home," Rachel called after her. "And I'm calling your mum to say you're on the way and to watch for you!"

Eva lifted her hand over her head in a backward wave. She hurried out of the hotel door and down the steps, gulping in the cool night air. She was determined not to cry and instead let her anger wash over her as she set off at a quick pace along the road towards home. Rachel and Marcus needn't worry. No criminal would dare mess with her the way she was feeling right now.

* * * *

Damon stood blinking as Eva was gone, melting into the crowd. *What the hell just happened?* It seemed like she'd given him a come-on then just walked off. He tried to spot her but couldn't, so he went out to see if she'd gone to the toilet. Maybe she'd felt ill? She did seem pretty tipsy. She'd been overtly flirty with him and she normally wasn't like that.

He waited outside the loos for a bit, then decided if she was in there, she'd been gone so long that something was wrong. So he decided to fetch Rachel and Jane to go into the toilets and check on her. He rounded the corner into reception and thought he saw her leaving through a crowd of people, so he shouted her name but there was no response. *Maybe it wasn't her.*

He headed back into the party and over to the table where the others had been sitting. The guys weren't there, but the girls were. Rachel was speaking to Jane, both with concern on their faces. They looked at him as he approached, and it might've been his imagination, but neither of them seemed pleased to see him.

He reached the table. "Have you seen Eva? She disappeared and I'm not sure what's going on."

"She's gone home," Rachel said.

He frowned, anxiety rising and driving up his heart rate. "Home? Why? Is she walking on her own?"

Rachel folded her arms. "We don't know why. We thought you could tell us." She threw her head back in a nod towards a group of people. Damon glanced over. It was a group of men with Tracey McKenna laughing loudly in the middle.

He frowned. What did that mean? His anxiety spiked. *What if it's something to do with why she was tearful at the movies?* "I'm going after her," he told them.

"She wants to be alone," Rachel said.

"I need to talk to her," Damon replied.

"If you upset her any more, you'll have me to answer to," Rachel said.

Guilt stabbed him in the gut. "She's upset because of *me*?"

Jane must've registered his concern because she softened. "We don't really know, to be honest. She didn't say why. But maybe it's a good idea for you to go after her and sort it out. Plus, we are a bit worried about her walking alone. She wouldn't let anyone go with her."

Damon nodded. "Okay." He turned and set off through reception and out of the front door. Then, as he hit the pavement, he began to run.

Chapter Fifteen

Eva walked the last leg towards home, kicking at sticks and stones along the way. "Fucking bloody bastard. They're all the bloody same."

After Rachel's SOS call, her mum and also more than likely her dad would be up waiting for her. She'd be treated to a healing cup of tea — and maybe even a biscuit this time. She smiled through her pain.

Eva passed by the neighbour's and spotted her parents' downstairs lights shining brightly. The kettle was bound to be on. She turned onto the driveway. Footsteps sounded on the pavement behind her, coming at quite a pace.

Her simmering temper erupted. Whoever it was must be up to no good at that time of night and they were going to get what was coming to them, courtesy of her right hook. She spun around to face the unknown ne'er-do-well and Damon rounded the corner, colliding with her. She grabbed his forearms to prevent being knocked off her feet.

"What the hell?" Eva said. "What're you doing here?"

He was breathing so hard that he couldn't answer at first. "What do you mean what am *I* doing here? I came to find you. Why did you bolt all of a sudden?"

Anger pierced her insides. "All of a sudden? Nothing about tonight was sudden."

He frowned. "What d'you mean?"

She rolled her eyes. "Do you really want me to spell it out?"

He shook his head. "You'll have to, because I have no idea what's going on."

Eva released his arms and threw her hands into the air. "Fine! I'm bloody tired of all your crap. That's what's going on. You act like you find me attractive with all your little compliments, but then you're quick to back off or point out that we're just friends. I've no idea where I stand with you and it's driving me crazy."

"Eva—"

"I keep hoping that something might happen between us, but you're blowing hot and cold all the time and it's so confusing. I'm happy to be your friend but I want more than that, and I deserve to know whether or not you want it too."

"Eva—"

"*And*, if you do just want friendship, then you should have the courtesy to say so and stop leading me on. And don't lie to me saying that you aren't interested in Tracey McKenna then be all over her like a rash."

"Eva, listen—"

"The thing is I thought it was really shitty of you to kiss me the other night then say you regretted it."

"*What*?"

"If you don't like me enough for things to go any further, then you shouldn't even be kissing me in the first place."

She pointed her finger and tapped him on the chest. "I deserve some respect. Either you find me attractive and want to kiss me and do other things to and with me, or you just want to be friends and not do any of those things. You can't have it both ways and —"

Damon circled her waist and drew her in, lifting his hand to her face.

Her voice faltered. *What's happening?*

He searched her eyes with a fierce intensity that pierced her soul and halted every train of thought. He stroked her cheek. "Of course I want more. I thought it was obvious."

Her pulse gathered pace, throbbing in her ears. She held her breath, terrified that he'd change his mind.

Damon closed the gap between them. He kissed her softly, parting her lips and sliding his tongue against hers. Her head started to swim, and she teetered on her heels. She couldn't believe it was finally happening.

Damon steadied her, manoeuvring her backward a few steps until they were pressed against the side of the house. They could have been up against the living room window for all Eva cared. She just didn't want him to stop.

She tangled her fingers in his hair. It was so soft, just as she'd imagined. He rubbed his thumb along her jawline and stroked his other hand down her spine, causing her to shiver uncontrollably. *Is this real or am I dreaming?*

She let out an involuntary moan as he trailed his mouth onto her neck. The sound seemed to spur him on, and he pressed against her, sliding his hand onto the back of her thigh.

"Is this okay?" he whispered against her skin.

Eva drew back to look into his eyes. "More than okay." She grasped his shirt and pulled him back in.

He groaned as the movement caused his fingers to graze up her thigh onto the lace of her underwear. "Eva," he murmured, "I want you so badly."

She shuddered with desire. Goosebumps erupted over every surface and her nerve endings sparked with fire.

She kissed him urgently, struggling to control her breathing. She was so consumed by her need for him that she barely registered the porch light flick on. It was followed by the sound of a key turning in the front door. They both startled, their lips breaking contact but bodies frozen in the same position.

"What was that?" Damon said.

Eva's eyes widened. "Shit. It's my parents. Rachel said she was going to phone ahead to tell them I was on my way. They'll be coming out to find me."

Damon searched her face. "I have to see you tomorrow. There's stuff we need to talk about." He paused to kiss her. "And stuff we need to do," he murmured against her lips.

"Damon," she whispered.

Another noise came from within the house. Damon disentangled himself then started backing away along the driveway, not taking his eyes off hers.

"Tomorrow," he said. "Come round to mine."

"In the morning?" she asked.

He paused at the edge of the driveway. "As soon as you're up." He looked meaningfully into her eyes. "I'll see you tomorrow."

Eva swallowed hard. "See you tomorrow."
Then he disappeared around the corner.

Chapter Sixteen

Eva opened the front door. Her dad was in the hallway, getting his shoes on.

"There you are." He smiled. "The search party, aka *moi*, was about to be deployed."

"Sorry. It's slow going, walking in these heels," Eva said.

Matthew gave her a knowing smile. "That's okay. Come through so your mother can give you the third degree. I mean...have a general conversation with you."

"Sounds great," Eva said with a look of mock dread on her face. She followed him along the hallway, wondering what was behind that smile he'd just given her. She tapped out a quick message to say she was home and all was well then sent it to both Rachel and Jane.

The tea had indeed been brewed and the three of them sat in the kitchen, sipping away. Meena asked how the evening had been and Eva played it down, saying it'd been 'fine' and everyone had had a good time.

"I just decided to leave early because I'd had too much to drink," she said.

Matthew nodded. "Good idea."

"Did Damon enjoy it?" Meena asked.

"Yes," Eva replied. She smiled, deciding to mess with her mum. "He seemed to particularly enjoy Tracey's company."

Meena's face fell. Guilt stabbed in Eva's chest, followed quickly by a resurgence of the nausea she'd experienced upon witnessing Tracey hanging off him. She'd been so distracted by that kiss that she'd never managed to ask him what had gone on.

Matthew frowned for some reason. Was he in on the matchmaking thing too? She remembered how much *she* and Damon had just been enjoying each other's company only a few yards away, and heat started rising in her face. She cleared her throat. "I'm pretty beat." She stood. "Night all."

She took herself off to bed.

All night she tossed and turned, the scene with Damon playing over in a loop in her mind. She looked at the clock — *six a.m.* How early had he meant for her to go over? He'd seemed keen that it be as soon as possible, but he might feel differently now. What if he regretted it again? Eva took a deep breath. *Stop overthinking.* She'd find out what he'd wanted to tell her soon enough from his own mouth.

His mouth. Eva remembered the way it had felt against hers and on her neck. *Stop it. Try to go back to sleep.* She lay down but her thoughts continued to race. What had gone on between Damon and Tracey the previous night? She should've given him the chance to explain rather than her going off on a rant. *Too much bloody wine.*

The next time she glanced at her clock, she'd only managed to get to six-thirty. She sighed, threw off the covers and went to climb in the shower. Once in there, all she could think about was the feel of Damon's hand on her thigh, sliding up her dress. It was driving her crazy. She wasn't sure she was going to manage to sit and listen to whatever he had to say without wanting to tear his clothes off. She climbed out of the shower and walked back into her bedroom wearing her towel. Her phone lit up with a message.

Hurry up.

So he *was* awake. She messaged back.

Just out of shower will throw on clothes and come straight over.

Don't tell me that. Now imagining you naked out of the shower.

Eva smiled.

Sorry. Better not tell you I'm putting on my new black underwear then.

You're killing me here!

Eva put on said underwear and added her press-stud blue shirt and a pair of jeans. She ran the hairdryer quickly over her hair, producing a pretty tousled result, but she didn't care. After brushing her teeth, she hurried downstairs, drank a glass of water and went out to the car.

Eva was beside herself with nerves on the drive over with potential scenarios playing out in her mind, all of which involved her and Damon ripping off each other's clothes. She shook her head to clear it and completed the drive with clenched teeth. As she pulled on his driveway, she rammed on the handbrake and unclicked the seatbelt.

He must've been watching for her because the door opened before she exited the car. She climbed out and nearly fell over at the sight of him. He was freshly showered with damp hair and bare feet, wearing light blue jeans and a white T-shirt. He wasn't even trying to do that jokey catalogue smoulder, but he had it down to a T. He leaned against the front door, the muscles in his arms flexed appealingly and his brown eyes burning into hers as she strode past him through the doorway. She stopped herself from grabbing and kissing him because she wouldn't want to stop, and there were things they needed to talk about first.

Eva went straight into the living room and turned to face him as he followed her through the doorway. The look in his eyes set her on fire and she tried to steady her breathing.

He stopped a few feet away from her. His voice was gravelly. "I'm not coming any closer because I know I'm not going to be able to control myself, and there're some things I need to tell you before I get carried away like I did last night."

Eva nodded and stayed silent. She put her hands behind her back to stop herself from reaching out for him.

Damon ran a hand through his hair. "Bloody hell, I don't even know where to start now." He took a deep breath in, and out again. "Okay. First of all, I don't suppose I need to explain now that *of course* I'm attracted to you. I can't stop thinking about you and I absolutely want this to be more than friendship. To be honest, I thought you knew because I've had trouble controlling my feelings. And I was only holding back because we've become good friends and I didn't want to wreck that, especially when I didn't know how you felt about me and I thought you still weren't over Callum."

He took another breath. Eva put her hand up as if asking permission to speak.

Damon laughed. He put on a stern teacher voice. "Yes, Eva?"

She smiled. "Please, sir, I am most definitely over Callum." She was relieved that humour went some way to dispelling the unbelievable sexual tension building in the room. It was almost as if she could reach out and grab it.

He smiled. "Great to know, thanks." But the heat was still burning in his eyes. "So second of all, *nothing* happened with Tracey last night. She came over and grabbed me, but I never so much as touched her. I just spent ages trying to get away from her, and in the end, I pretended I needed to go to the toilet." He screwed up his face. "That's when I saw you being slimed on by Eric. And thirdly, I've no idea what you were talking about when you said I kissed you and regretted it. I don't remember kissing you at all. I assume this was that night I was blind drunk and you brought me home?"

Eva nodded.

"My memory of that night is patchy, to say the least," he said. "I wish I could remember kissing you, but I don't. However, I certainly remember doing it last night and I do not regret a thing about it…except getting disturbed by your parents."

She leaned back against the wall, trying not to interrupt him by grabbing hold of him in a fit of passion.

He moved towards her. "Or maybe it was a good thing we were disturbed, because the way I was feeling last night, I don't think I would've wanted to stop at kissing."

He was right in front of her, his eyes dark with longing and burning into hers. Eva tried to summon the power of speech but failed. They stood for a moment, a couple of inches apart. She grasped his shirt and pulled him in. The cold light of day had done nothing to take the heat out of their situation and their kiss quickly became fevered.

Eva slid her tongue into his mouth, and he groaned in response, sending a delicious thrill into her core. He pressed her against the wall, and she wrapped her arms around his neck, drawing him deeper.

He broke off to cup her face. "Are you sure this is what you want? I feel like it's come out of nowhere."

Nowhere? I've wanted this for over a decade. She gazed into his eyes. "I'm sure."

The corner of his mouth flickered in a smile and he leaned back into their kiss. He lifted her and she wrapped her legs around his waist, kissing him as he manoeuvred them towards the sofa.

He collapsed them onto it. She revelled in the feeling of his weight on top of her, holding her securely and sparking every nerve ending in her body. He kissed her in a way that conveyed a deep sense of longing, like he was trying to drink in everything about her, like he'd been waiting just as long as she had for it to happen. *But there's no way that can be right.*

He slid his hand to the top of her shirt and popped the top stud. A wave of exhilaration surged through her body.

He popped a second stud and a third. The anticipation was killing her. Why didn't he just rip it open? She didn't care if it tore. He brushed his hands against her skin as he worked his way down, causing an unbearable ache to build deep in her belly.

The shirt hung open but her skin was on fire, despite the cool air reaching it.

Damon slid one hand behind her head and ran the other along her neck, pushing her bra strap off her shoulder.

She breathed his name as he kissed her. He slid his lips down her neck, sucking her skin gently against his teeth. Eva began to tremble. He kissed along the length of her collarbone and began to drag his mouth lower still.

The doorbell rang, and they both froze.

"*Shit,*" Damon said. He lifted his head, listening as if he were hoping whoever it was would disappear. The doorbell went again.

Damon groaned. "You've *got* to be kidding me." He leaned forward and rested his forehead against Eva's. He met her eyes, his voice low. "Maybe they'll go away."

Eva shook her head. "It's seven-forty-five in the morning. It must be something important."

Damon swore and dragged himself to his feet. Eva sat up and pulled her clothing back together, quickly re-snapping her shirt.

Whoever it was started hammering at the door. Eva's heart rate picked up and she shot Damon a worried look as he left the room. She listened, wondering who it could be.

She heard him open the door. "Sarah?" he said.

There were footsteps, and Adele and Sam appeared through the door.

Adele's eyes lit up and she came over. "Can you help me take my coat off? I can't get the zip."

"Of course," Eva said as she tended to the jacket. She turned to Sam to give him a hand. She could hear Sarah's voice from the doorstep. She was speaking quickly and there was a distressed tone to her voice.

"The ambulance is on the way to the hospital," Sarah said. "I'm really sorry, but I don't have anyone else to leave them with. Mum is riding with him in the ambulance and I want to meet them there."

"It's fine, really. Just go. I hope everything is okay," Damon said.

There were tears in Sarah's voice. "Me too."

Eva turned to Adele. "Has something happened?"

Adele nodded. "Grandpa went to sleep and fell over, so Grandma has to take him to hospital to get better. Mummy is going to go help wake him up, so me and Sam are with Daddy for a sleepover."

Eva tucked a stray strand of Adele's hair behind her ear. "That sounds like a good plan. I bet Grandpa will be better soon. The doctors at the hospital are very good. Did I tell you about how they fixed my leg?" Eva tried to drown out the worried conversation between the kids' parents, and in the meantime put the TV onto Sam's favourite cartoon channel. She lifted him onto her lap and he watched contentedly.

Adele chatted away about what she'd been doing at school and Eva interjected with questions and interested noises. Damon entered the room with a deep frown on his face, which softened when he saw Eva sitting calmly with the kids.

"Eva" — he was clearly controlling his voice — "can I have a quick word with you in the kitchen?"

"Yeah, sure." Eva deposited Sam next to Adele and followed Damon into the next room.

He turned round to face her. "I'm really sorry about all this."

"It's okay, honestly," she said.

Damon took a deep breath. "Sarah's dad was taken unwell this morning and they're on their way to hospital. It sounds really bad."

Eva nodded. "I'm really sorry. I hope he's all right."

Damon sighed. "I hope so too."

She reached out to touch his arm.

He met her gaze. "It seems we keep getting interrupted."

Eva remembered what had been happening in the living room only a few minutes before and heat rose in her face. Damon reached out and circled her waist. She stepped into him and wrapped her arms around his neck.

His grazed his lips against her ear. "I don't want you to go."

"You should have some time on your own with the kids," Eva said as she trailed her fingers through his hair. "Keep some normalcy. They'll have sensed the stress and be worried about it."

He leaned back. "Can I see you tomorrow?"

"Of course," Eva said. "But won't you still have the kids?"

"Sarah's coming to collect them after dinner tomorrow. She doesn't want them staying any longer or it'll disrupt their routine," Damon said.

"Okay." She stroked his face. "Just text me with what time you want me."

He leaned in to kiss her. "I want you all the time."

She kissed him back but after a few seconds pulled away and gently moved out of his arms.

"I'd better go," she said. "But I'll see you tomorrow."

Damon sighed. "Okay." He took her hand to lead her to the door.

Eva gave Damon a brief hug and a kiss, told the kids goodbye then exited for the car. He stayed in the doorway to wave her off as she drove away.

On the drive home, Eva tried to make sense of everything that had just happened. It was turning out to be a rollercoaster. One minute she was in despair that she'd never be with Damon in the way she wanted. The next it seemed as if she'd get everything she wished for, then yet again it seemed that the fates were against them. She remembered the distress in Sarah's voice and a wave of empathy washed over her. Poor Sarah... She must be so worried about her dad. Eva hoped they got him to the hospital in time and that he'd recover.

Her thoughts shifted to Damon's tortured expression when he'd told her what'd happened, and the way she'd heard him comforting Sarah on the doorstep. There must still be significant feelings involved on his part. Her heart sank. It was out in the open that Damon was attracted to her, but his heart clearly laid elsewhere. That meant Eva could never truly get everything she wanted. She forced herself to stop thinking about it. She was being selfish in these ruminations when Sarah's dad was ill. She should be grateful that she might be able to have a small part of Damon, even if she couldn't have him all to herself.

Chapter Seventeen

Eva awoke from a nap, still exhausted from the late night, getting up early, the excitement of seeing Damon and *nearly* fulfilling her teenage fantasy—then having her hopes dashed yet again.

Her phone started ringing and her heart lifted. It was Damon's number on a video call.

"Hey," he said, "I've been thinking about you."

She smiled. "What've you been thinking?"

He grinned. "I'll show you tomorrow night."

Eva laughed. "Sounds good."

Damon leaned back. "What've you been doing?"

"Not much. Calling Rachel and Jane to assure them I'm not spiralling into depression over a guy."

He raised his eyebrows. "Which guy? Should I be worried?"

She smiled. "Just this handsome dude with brown hair and come-to-bed eyes."

He puffed out his chest, smiling. "I'll need to sort him out." He let out his breath. "Seriously though, are they still on the warpath with me? I reckon Rachel's got a mean left hook."

Eva laughed. "You're not wrong there. But no, it's fine. I explained what really happened with Tracey…and the rest of it."

He gave her a meaningful look. "The rest of it?"

Heat rose in her face. "Not the details. Just an overview."

He smiled. "We'll fill in the details tomorrow."

Eva nodded. She could still feel the blush in her cheeks. She sat a bit straighter. "Have you got any news about Sarah's dad?"

"Yeah," he said. "He's had a heart attack but got there in time to get some treatment. He's in coronary care."

"That's good," Eva said. "Is he stable?"

"Yes," Damon said. "I hope he's okay. He's a lovely man."

Eva studied his sad expression. He must miss Sarah's family almost as much as he missed her. She was sad for him and also for herself, because if he still felt that deeply about Sarah then her own chances of having a serious relationship with him were low. *Stop being selfish.* "Is there anything I can do to help?"

He smiled. "Seeing you is all I want."

A warm glow settled in her chest. Whatever was developing between them was still more than she could've hoped for. Even if it was just a casual fling, that was better than the perpetual longing she'd harboured for years. She smiled. "What time shall I come over tomorrow?"

"The kids are getting collected at six." He smiled. "So one minute past six?"

She laughed. "I'll come at six-thirty to give you time to get yourself spruced up."

Eva went downstairs to forage for some food. Her mum was in the kitchen. Meena placed a full plate onto the table. "There you go. Eat that. It'll sort out your wine hangover."

"I'm not hungover," Eva said, then found that her head *was* a bit sore and she was starving. "Okay, maybe a little." She started tucking into her food.

Meena sat across from her with her own plate. "Is everything alright after last night?"

Eva frowned, wondering what that meant. Then she remembered what she'd told her mum the previous evening about Damon and Tracey. "Oh, yeah. I'm fine, thanks." She took another forkful and mulled over how much to tell. She didn't want Meena to get the wrong idea and have her and Damon married off in her mind. She swallowed. "Nothing happened with Damon and Tracey last night. I got the wrong end of the stick. And I'm going to see him tomorrow."

The corner of Meena's mouth flickered. "Oh yes? Another friends' get together?"

Eva hesitated. "I think we're becoming more than friends."

Meena didn't do a good job of suppressing her joy. She smiled broadly and poured them both some tea from the flowery teapot. "I knew it."

Eva sighed. "Don't get over-excited. It's nothing serious. I think he's still in love with Sarah."

Meena shook her head. "Nonsense."

"Mum," Eva said, "I'm telling you. Don't make this into a bigger deal than it is. You'll end up disappointed."

Meena glanced at her. "As long as it's not you who ends up disappointed."

Eva smiled. "I'll be fine. I've been toughened over the last few months."

Meena touched her hand, a pained look in her eyes. "I know. And I don't want you hurt anymore." She stirred her tea. "I just want you to be happy. That's why I'm trying to help."

"I know," Eva said. "But you can't arrange my love life for me. And you were the one who turned down an arranged marriage in order to marry Dad, don't forget."

"I'm not arranging a marriage for you. I'm trying to help steer you towards true love." Meena smiled. "That's what I have with your father, and I want it for both my daughters too."

Eva shook her head, smiling. "You can't force Damon to love me. None of us have control over that emotion."

Meena eyed her and Eva realised that her previous statement was easy to read into. She'd said that Damon couldn't be forced to love her, but she hadn't mentioned anything about her feelings towards him. They were fast getting out of control and she needed to protect herself.

* * * *

After what seemed like an eternity rather than a little over twenty-four hours, the next evening rolled around and Eva got ready to head out to Damon's. She deliberated over what to wear but then decided it didn't really matter, because she was rather hoping that whatever she had on would be removed soon after her arrival.

Her nerves weren't jangling quite so much on the drive over, having been in the same situation the morning before. She wondered how Sarah's dad was doing and if there'd be any more of an update on him.

Eva parked and got out of the car. Something appeared out of place. The front door didn't seem properly shut. As she approached, she discovered that was indeed the case. *That's weird.* Although Damon knew she was coming, so maybe he'd left it open. *Maybe when I open it, he'll be there in his underwear – or nothing at all.* Eva shivered in anticipation. She pushed open the door, shutting it quietly behind her. There were voices in the living room. *Who's he with?* She walked along the hallway and peered into the room just in time to see Tracey McKenna throw her arms around Damon's neck.

A shock of pain stabbed her in the gut and she turned and ran down the hallway and out of the front door. Bile rose into the back of her throat as a vision replayed of arriving home in Edinburgh and being confronted by a similar scene.

Eva ran to the car, got in and started it. She reversed off the driveway at speed, tears blinding her as she roared off along the road.

Chapter Eighteen

The front door slammed. Damon pushed Tracey off him. "What the *hell* do you think you're doing?"

She frowned. "What do you think? Come here and I'll show you..." She started to move towards him again.

He held up his hand. "Don't come anywhere near me."

She folded her arms, her mouth set in a thin line. "I can't remember you complaining last time."

He threw his hands in the air. "Last time I was sixteen years old and you threw me into a bush. I'm now thirty years old and this is *my* house." He gestured towards the front door. "I'm telling you to get the hell out."

She put her hands on her hips. "You can't be serious. Anyone else would be delighted to be in your position."

"I'm not anyone else, so piss off."

Tracey gritted her teeth. "*Fine.* It's your loss." She turned and lashed out her hand, sending a table lamp crashing to the ground as she stalked out of the house. The door slammed behind her.

Damon drew breath. *What the hell was that?* He'd been quickly tidying, awaiting Eva's arrival, and when the doorbell went, he figured she was here early. He'd opened the door expectantly and been disappointed to see Tracey standing there, dolled up to the nines. He was thrown, and she'd used the opportunity to march past him into the house. When he'd gone into the living room after her, she'd said something like '*This is your lucky night*' and thrown herself at him. The next thing he heard before he got chance to push her off him was the door slamming. *Could that have been Eva arriving and departing?* Had she seen Tracey with her arms around him in that split second before he'd thrown her off? Damon groaned. Of course she had. He grabbed his wallet and searched for his car keys. *Where the hell are they?*

He checked the coffee table and in the kitchen before coming back into the living room and finding them under one of the sofa cushions. He cursed under his breath, *a valuable few minutes wasted*. He hurried out of the front door and got into the car to drive to Eva's.

When Damon pulled onto the drive, his heart sank. Her car wasn't there. *Where is she? At Rachel's? Or Jane's?* He sat for a moment, trying to think where to go next.

He decided to go ask Meena where Eva might be. It was possible he'd get a slap in the face if Eva had recounted what she'd seen to her mum, but he might figure out her whereabouts more quickly, so it'd be worth it.

Damon stood on the doorstep and rang the bell, feeling nauseated Eva's mum answered the door.

"Hi, Auntie Meena." He waited for her to punch him or slam the door in his face. Instead she smiled and gestured for him to enter.

"Come through," Meena said. "I'm afraid Eva isn't here, but you and I need to have a little chat."

Damon's nausea intensified.

He sat on the kitchen chair that was offered, and Meena set about pouring them some tea. He smiled, thinking about what Eva had told him about her mum's tea obsession and how it was her go-to in any stressful situation. But then that thought made him even more nervous. If the tea was out, then the conversation must be headed towards bad news. Meena set a mug in front of him, and he grasped it with both hands.

She sat across from him. "I need to tell you a story. This is in the strictest confidence, because I know Eva hasn't told anyone except Matthew and me yet. But I also know she would've told you when she was ready, so I'm not breaking her confidence really. And goodness knows you two need all the help you can get."

Damon couldn't argue with that.

Meena sipped her tea. "This is difficult for me to tell because it breaks my heart, but at least we have the tea to soothe us. It's chamomile."

Damon smiled.

Meena continued. "Eva and Callum were in love — or so Eva thought. But things hit a rough patch at work and it impacted her personal life. She was unbearably stressed over a long period. Unfortunately, Callum couldn't handle it. At the very time he should've been supporting my daughter, he was pulling away." Meena set her mouth in a grim line. "Eva tried to confide in him, but he wasn't interested. He started making excuses about working late and saying they'd talk later. Then one night she came home from work early and found him in the living room, rolling round naked with his secretary, Hannah."

Meena looked at Damon. A new tidal wave of nausea crashed over him. Eva had found him in what might've appeared to be a similar situation with Tracey.

Damon rubbed his face then put his head in his hands. "I'm assuming Eva told you she walked in on Tracey and me."

Meena nodded.

He lifted his head. "What happened tonight was a big misunderstanding. Nothing has happened between Tracey and me. She barged in and tried it on but I threw her out." He sighed. "Eva just happened to witness the wrong two seconds." He leaned back. "But this thing with Callum makes it a whole lot worse."

Meena sipped her tea. "I know. It has coloured the way she sees everything…even herself."

Damon paused, something was niggling at the back of his mind. "What was stressing Eva at the time?"

Meena shifted in her seat, averting her gaze. "It's not something she's keen on talking about." She cleared her throat and met his eyes again. "When something really traumatizes her, she buries it deeply. It really isn't good for her."

Damon could tell Meena knew more than she was letting on. But she'd already told him one secret and it wasn't fair to push for another. He'd try to find out eventually but currently there were more immediate issues to be dealt with. "I need to see her. Do you know where she is?"

Meena nodded. "Yes, and I think it'd be a good idea for you to set the record straight. She doesn't need any more stress right now. After she got in, she was really upset and gave me a quick gist of why."

Damon squirmed slightly in his seat.

Meena continued. "Then she called Jane and asked to come see her at work. She didn't want to go to Rachel's in a state with the kids being there."

Damon's heart swelled. It was typical of Eva to put the wellbeing of Rachel's kids ahead of her own need for comfort. "She's gone to Alton Hall now?"

Meena nodded.

Damon got to his feet. "Thanks for the tea — and for confiding in me." He turned to go and Meena followed him to the front door.

Damon paused in the doorway. "I'm not like Callum, you know. I'd never hurt Eva."

"I know, because I've known you since you were two years old." Meena smiled. "That's why we've had this conversation. Now go find my daughter."

Damon didn't need telling twice. He jumped in his car and drove up the road in record time.

Once he arrived at Alton Hall, he headed directly for the spa and asked for Jane. The woman at the desk went to find her. Damon paced the area. He was aware that a couple of people were giving him funny looks, but he didn't care.

A couple of minutes later Jane appeared with a wary expression on her face. Despite that, Damon held out hope that she'd be willing to listen.

"Hi," Jane said. "What're you doing here?"

"I'm trying to find Eva. Do you know where she is?"

Jane stayed silent, appraising him.

"Listen," Damon said. "I know you don't have any reason to trust me, but could I have a private word with you to explain myself?"

Jane narrowed her eyes. Then she nodded in the direction of the spa office behind the reception desk.

She led him in and closed the door behind them. "Go on."

Damon told Jane everything that'd happened since his kids had been collected that evening. She listened intently, nodding at intervals.

Just before he got to the part about Meena telling him what had happened between Eva and Callum, he paused. He wasn't sure if Eva had confided in Jane about it and didn't want to break Meena or Eva's confidence.

Jane smiled, clearly interpreting his hesitation. "It's okay. When Eva got here, she told me about walking in on Callum and Hannah."

Damon finished the story. "I really need to see her and explain it was just a misunderstanding. I can't stand her thinking I'd do something like that to her."

Jane nodded. "I believe you."

Relief washed over him.

"I'll tell you where she is," Jane said, "but it'll be up to her if she wants to listen or not. I'm sure she will, though. She was just shocked and had a knee-jerk reaction because of what she's been through with Callum."

"Thanks." He sighed. "I hope you're right."

"After Eva got here, we talked," Jane said "She was really upset and I didn't want her driving home, so I called in a favour and got her booked into one of the hotel suites. I told her to get a hot bath and I've had some nice wine sent to the room. I was planning on going to see her after my shift to share it with her, but if you play your cards right, you could be the one drinking it instead."

Damon's stomach churned. What if she slammed the door in his face? But he had to try. "Okay. What room is it?"

"It's two hundred and twenty-six, on the second floor," Jane said. "I'll call her to let her know you're coming and tell her I think she should listen — and so does her mum."

Damon left the area and went to the bank of elevators in the main reception, riding the lift to the second floor. Room two hundred and twenty-six was set farther into the hotel and relatively hard to find, but he figured it gave Jane more time to speak to Eva and pave the way for him.

He arrived at the room, knocked on the door and prayed, his heart pounding. It opened and he held his breath, breathing a sigh of relief when it didn't slam shut again.

"Hi," Eva said.

"Hi. Did Jane call you?"

"Yes." Eva gestured behind her where the sound of water running was apparent. "I only just caught the call because I was running the bath."

"Can I come in?" he asked.

He could see her weighing it up, her previous experience telling her not to trust him because of what Callum had done, but the fact that her best friend and her mum did trust him told her to give him the benefit of the doubt.

She stood to one side. "Okay."

He entered the room.

Eva closed the door behind him. "I'll just go and stop the bath, otherwise we'll be swimming out of here."

She went into the bathroom. The suite was huge. There was a four-poster bed in the main area and, underneath the large bay window, a bottle of sparkling wine was chilling in an ice bucket. The water stopped running and Eva came back through.

She leaned against the bedpost, a few yards away from him. "Do you want a drink?"

"No thanks. I just need to get this all out," Damon said.

"Okay," she said.

Damon took a deep breath. "I know you walked into the house before and saw Tracey." His mouth soured as he said her name. "But it wasn't what it seemed. Do you remember me telling you about how she was all over me at the reunion and I was trying to get rid of her?"

Eva nodded.

"At the time, I didn't really think about it but she was asking me where I lived. So I told her the street name but not the number. Then she was asking what kind of car I drive. So I reckon she must've driven along the street searching for my car. Anyway, when I opened the door, I was expecting to see *you* standing there. Boy was I disappointed."

The corner of Eva's mouth flickered in a smile, giving him hope.

He drew breath. "She barged her way in and threw herself at me again. Unfortunately, I think that was the split second you walked in. If you'd stayed any longer, you would've seen me telling her to piss off."

Eva smiled openly. "You literally said 'piss off'?"

He blew out a sigh of relief at the sight of her smile. "Yes."

Eva laughed. "I bet she really *was* pissed off."

He smiled. "Yeah, but I don't give a crap. All I care about is what *you* think."

"I believe you," she said. "When Jane called, she also said that she spoke quickly to her friend Martina while you were on your way up. She's the one who's a mutual friend of Tracey's, and Martina confirmed that Tracey called her to badmouth you about rejecting her."

"Eva…" Damon groaned. "You could've told me that before and put me out of my misery."

"Nah, this was much more fun." Eva grinned. "You should've heard what Martina said Tracey called you, friend for life there, Damo."

Damon laughed. "She can call me whatever the hell she wants. I'm just glad she got the message." He looked at her. "I'm sorry I wasn't more firm with her at the reunion. If I hadn't tried to let her down gently, she would've realised I wasn't interested. Then tonight never would've happened."

Eva smiled. "You don't have to apologise for being a nice guy, Damon. It's not your fault Tracey's a bunny-boiling narcissist. And I'm sorry too. I shouldn't have jumped to conclusions. I'm a bit paranoid these days."

Damon hesitated. He needed to tell her that Meena had confided in him about Callum.

Eva eyed him. "What is it?"

He ran a hand through his hair. "I spoke to your mum before."

She nodded. "Jane said."

"Did she tell you that Meena told me about you walking in on Callum?"

Eva took a deep breath. "Yeah. It's okay. I was going to tell you. I just didn't know how to say it. It's pretty humiliating."

He closed the gap between them and drew her into a hug.

She nestled her face on his chest.

The tension poured out of him. It seemed to somehow clear his senses. He'd been so distracted by his stress that he hadn't fully taken in an important detail.

Eva was wearing only a bathrobe.

He drew back to study her. *What's underneath? Underwear? Nothing?* He met her gaze and could tell she knew exactly what he was thinking. He flicked his gaze behind her towards the four-poster bed and back again.

The look in her eyes sent heat firing through him. "Damon…"

He lifted his hands to undo her robe tie, his mind racing in anticipation. She held his gaze as he slid his hands under the shoulders of the robe and pushed the material off. It fell around her bare feet.

Damon lowered his eyes. She was wearing a black lacy bra and briefs, and the material had a sheer quality to it.

His heart hammered in his chest, making it difficult for him to catch his breath. He stood frozen for a second, unable to believe it might finally happen. Eva pulled him in and kissed him. He slid his arms around her, the feel of her bare skin sending shock waves of excitement through his entire body.

Eva drew him towards the bed and lifted his T-shirt over his head. She slid her hands over his chest and up behind his head, drawing him back into her kiss. He groaned as she trailed her mouth down his neck, waves of tingling electricity breaking out over his skin and sending a direct line of fiery heat into his loins.

He was aware of the rest of his clothing falling away until only his underwear was left. There was a buzzing in his ears and the air around him seemed heavy and thick.

Eva reached towards his briefs.

"Wait," he said, taking her hands. "I need to tell you something."

She groaned. "Oh God, what now?"

"No, it's nothing bad," he said, then hesitated. "At least I hope it isn't."

"What is it?" she asked, planting butterfly kisses all over his face.

He tried to summon the power of coherent speech as the touch of her lips fused his thought processes.

"I just don't want you to be disappointed." He took a deep breath. "It's been... Well it's been a while for me. And I've been wanting this with you for so long I might not be able to contain myself."

Eva paused her kisses to meet his gaze and he got lost in the green hue of her eyes. "You could never disappoint me. It doesn't matter if the first time is a bit quicker. Just think of it as an appetizer."

Fireworks went off in his brain, rooting him to the spot.

She ran her hands down his body and slid off his underwear, then pushed him onto the bed. He leaned on his elbows and she crawled over him, his pulse whooshing in his ears. *Is this finally happening?* He glanced at the door, afraid someone was going to hammer on it or burst through in keeping with their previous track record. But nothing happened.

Eva leaned to kiss him, her hair showering softly around his face. She smelled like heaven.

She whispered in his ear. "You can just let go. It doesn't matter. We've got all night."

A shock of excitement fired through him and Damon was concerned it could be game over there and then if he weren't careful. He closed his eyes for a moment to collect himself, then slid his hands down her body, removing the lacy material as he went.

He revelled in the feeling of her naked body on top of him, her skin grazing his and setting every fibre in his being alight. It wouldn't be long until he lost his senses, so he uttered the last rational thought in his mind before it was too late. "The condom. It's in my jeans pocket."

Eva held the packet aloft. "I got it." She tore it open and rolled it on.

Damon pushed his hands into her hair and held her head, keeping his eyes on hers as she slowly slid onto him. The sensations building inside him were so intense that they took his breath away. He felt like he'd wanted this forever. She started moving rhythmically on top of him and he brought her mouth down onto his. She moaned gently against his lips and his self-restraint started to waver.

Eva's movements became faster and more urgent. He relinquished all control to her, pleasure making his head swim. It wouldn't be long, she was fast unravelling him and he wanted to give in to it. But he tried to hold on as long as he could. He kissed her with a desperation that clearly conveyed his sense of abandonment. He was hers to do with as she pleased.

She slid her mouth across his cheek until her lips came to rest on his ear. "Damon, let go."

Liquid fire spread through his veins. He couldn't breathe.

"Evie," he moaned against her cheek, the last sliver of self-control slipping away. Pleasure exploded inside him. He pulled her into his body and surrendered to it, wave after wave rolling over him as he shuddered in her arms.

Damon held her tightly, trying to catch his breath. Her heart was beating against his chest, in time with his. He never wanted to let her go.

Eventually Eva lifted her head to pepper his face with kisses. "How was that?"

"Amazing," Damon breathed. "You're so amazing." He kissed her softly, trying to gather the strands of himself back together. He rested his forehead against hers. She had shattered him in a spectacular way.

Eva sank into him and he wrapped his arms around her.

He stroked her hair. "I can't believe it finally happened."

She sighed. "Me neither."

He breathed in the scent of her. It intoxicated him. As they lay there, he sensed her breathing start to change rhythm. "Eva?"

"Mmm?"

"You're not falling asleep, are you?"

"Yeah," she breathed. "You've exhausted me."

He lifted her head to look into her eyes. "You promised me 'all night'. In any case, you've not had your turn yet."

She frowned, then must've figured out what he meant because she smiled and kissed him. "As long as you're not too tired."

He flipped them over in one easy movement, so that she was underneath him. "No way."

He kissed her thoroughly, running his hand down her side then slowly trailing his fingers across her abdomen. Goosebumps rose against his fingertips.

She pushed her hands into his hair, sliding her tongue against his. Damon sensed her breathing start to alter as he reached between her thighs. He slowly began to tease her with his fingers. She arched her back to bring his touch deeper and a sweet thrill fired into his core.

He trailed his kisses slowly down her front, steadying her as she writhed with pleasure under him. By the time he'd worked his way to her lower abdomen, she was trembling. He inched his way to her most intimate areas, revelling in her moans as she raked her fingers through his hair. He wanted to make her feel good, make her cry out his name and beg him not to stop.

He tuned in to exactly what to do in order to intensify her groans of pleasure. She pushed his head deeper, and he could tell that she was getting close to losing control. He held her in position, mercilessly driving her harder and closer to the edge. Her breathing became laboured, and he sensed the first ripples of her climax start to roll over her. She called his name and he tried to imprint the sound of it in his mind. He stayed with her through the waves of her orgasm, intensifying her sensation right until the moment she sighed with satisfaction and stilled.

He climbed back up her body to kiss her. She wrapped her arms tightly around him and he let his weight sink onto her. He nuzzled his face into her neck, breathing her in.

She let out a deep sigh. "Okay. Now I can die happy."

He smiled against her neck. "Don't die, because then we won't get to do this again."

She stroked his hair. "Good point."

They lay in silence for a minute, then he lifted his head to kiss her. "Are you sure it's okay that your mum told me what happened with Callum? I feel bad that it didn't come from you."

She nodded. "I'm glad you know. Plus, it saves me the embarrassment of telling you myself." She stroked his face. "I mean, I'm only twenty-nine years old and my husband was already shagging a younger woman." She frowned. "I figured I must have zero sex appeal in order for that to happen."

Damon shook his head. "I can one hundred percent vouch that you are off the scale sexy, as demonstrated by what we've just done. The problem was with him and not you."

Eva's cheeks coloured and she smiled at him. "So you *do* think having brains and wearing glasses is sexy after all?"

He smiled, unable to believe that she had to ask that question. "Hell yes. I always have." He leaned to kiss her, murmuring against her lips, "I don't suppose you've got your glasses with you?"

Eva smiled against his mouth. "No, why?"

"Because you'd look really hot in them." He trailed his lips across her cheek to her ear. "I think I'd like you to wear them during sex. In fact, I know I would."

Eva laughed.

Damon studied her. He considered asking her about the other niggle at the back of his mind, the one that'd been there since he'd spoken to Meena earlier. He wondered what the stressful situation had been in the build up to her split with Callum. But he wanted Eva to confide in him in her own time, especially since she never got the chance to be the one to tell him the details about Callum.

"What did you do when you caught them together?" he asked quietly.

Eva grinned. "I threw them out of the house. Still naked."

Damon laughed. "Really?"

Eva nodded, still smiling. "Yep."

"It was way more than they deserved." He traced her lower lip with his thumb. "Shall we put more hot water in the bath, and take that wine in there?"

Eva smiled. "Good idea."

He lifted himself up, then pulled her to her feet. "I feel a second wave coming on. I've never had sex in a Jacuzzi bath before. Maybe it's time to cross that off the bucket list."

Chapter Nineteen

Eva awoke and for a split-second anxiety stabbed in her gut. *Was that a dream?* She lifted her head and Damon was leaning on one elbow watching her. She smiled, her memories of the night before washing away any unease.

Damon stroked her hair from her face. "Hi there." He leaned in to kiss her.

She traced the contours of his chest. Everything seemed so natural with him. Eva was struck by the lack of the self-consciousness that she remembered from her first time with Callum. It was like this was meant to be. Plus, she'd been so consumed by her passion for Damon that there was no room left for embarrassment. She'd even been the one to take the lead initially, which she'd never done the first time before. His admission of vulnerability had spurred her on to take over, and she'd been entirely comfortable in doing so.

Damon drew her in to kiss her more deeply, running his hand down her back and making her shiver.

She noticed the bedside clock over his shoulder. "Don't you have work today?"

He kissed her neck. "Why? What time is it?"

"After eight," Eva said.

He sat up. "Crap. I need to go. Are you off today?"

"Yes, it's a random health services bank holiday today," she said.

"Aw, man." He cupped her face. "I can't believe I have to leave you here like this. I just want to stay and carry on where we left off last night."

"I can come round to yours after work if you like," Eva said.

Damon's eyes lit up. "Yes, I'd most definitely like. I'll get in at six. Can you be there for then?"

She smiled. "On the dot."

He kissed her again, then with a groan, got up and put on his clothes. He sat on the bed to tend to his footwear and Eva propped herself on an elbow to rub his back. He stood and turned to kiss her goodbye and the duvet fell away from her.

Damon groaned again. "I don't know how I'm going to get through today with that image in my head."

She shrugged, smiling. "You'll see it all again later."

Damon kissed her and went to the door. He turned back. "Six p.m., on the dot."

Eva laughed. "See you then."

The door closed behind him and Eva lay back in the bed with a sigh. Then she realised her phone was alit with texts from Jane and also from Rachel. She picked up the phone to type a quick update to Jane. Then she started reading what Rachel had sent, but was interrupted by a message coming through from Damon.

There's a good chance I'll crash this bloody car because I can't stop thinking about you.

Concentrate and stop texting

Eva tended to her message to Rachel then jumped in the shower.

Once she got home, she had a cup of tea with her mum and explained about the reconciliation with Damon—minus many of the details, of course. She tried to hide her phone after it started buzzing with explicit messages from him. When she got to her room, she scrolled through to answer with her own X-rated content. She hoped he had his phone notifications switched off at work lest anyone saw what she'd written on his lock screen.

Finally, evening came and she set off to meet him at his house. When she arrived, she remembered the last time she'd been there and how much things had changed in twenty-four hours.

The door opened before she even reached it, and she practically jumped into his arms.

Damon smiled, reaching to touch the frame of her glasses. "You remembered."

Eva smiled. "Yes."

His gaze darkened as he looked at her mouth. He pushed the door shut behind her and kissed her. Eva pulled him in tightly. It seemed like they'd been apart for months rather than hours. Desire surged inside her. She needed him now.

He pressed her against the door and slid her skirt up, running his hands down to rip off her briefs and practically tearing them in his desperation. She fumbled at the fastening of his jeans, swearing in frustration before managing to push them to his knees.

Damon lifted her and she wrapped her legs around his hips. He fumbled quickly with a condom then drove into her, kissing her neck and chest as he moved rhythmically inside her.

Eva held his head against her neck as he thrust faster and harder. Her head swam with rapture. Damon shifted in order to stimulate her pleasure further and the sensations building in her belly swelled and intensified.

She gave into it, moaning his name and feeling him become caught up with her. He groaned against her chest, collapsing them against the door as their breathing started to slow again.

"God, we didn't even make it out of the hallway," he sighed against her skin.

"I know," she said. "It would've taken too long."

Damon pulled his clothing back on and lifted her into his arms to carry her to his bedroom where he undressed her fully, apart from the glasses, and they went in for round two.

Afterwards, Eva was revelling in the scent of him and the feel of his muscular form lying against her when his phone rang. Damon glanced at it, then back at Eva.

"Just answer it," Eva said. "It might be important."

He swung his legs out of bed and lifted his mobile to answer the call.

He covered the mouthpiece with his hand. "Sorry... It's Sarah."

Eva's heart sank and a wave of guilt washed over her for feeling that way. She covered it up by smiling and nodding at him.

He spoke softly on the phone, concern and care apparent in his voice. On one hand it was lovely that he was supportive of the mother of his children at such a difficult time, a real testament to his measure as a man. But on the other, she had to admit to her jealousy, because Damon clearly still cared about Sarah. *He must still be in love with her.* Eventually he ended the call and climbed back into bed.

Eva tried to pretend that she wasn't rattled. "Is everything okay? How's her dad?"

He nodded. "She was just calling with an update. He's making progress."

Relief at that news went some way to soothing her. "That's good. I hope he gets onto the general ward soon."

"Yes," Damon said. "They're going to see how he does over the next twenty-four hours."

"Are the kids okay?" Eva asked.

"Yeah, they seem to be." He paused. "I hope they aren't traumatized by the way it happened."

"I don't think so," Eva told him. "You and Sarah have done a good job of reassuring them and explaining things. I reckon they'll be just fine."

She studied him. There was a look on his face, something different to before. She wasn't sure what it was, but she figured he must've been thinking about Sarah.

"Come here," he said quietly, drawing her close. He stroked her hair. "Can you stay over tonight?"

"I'd like to," she said. "But I think I'd better stay at home after being away last night or Mum is going to go crazy and book us a wedding venue."

Damon laughed. "And *my* mum will be there with her, planning it all."

171

Eva was aware that she was doing it again. Building back up the internal wall that Damon had so far managed to break down. But she needed to protect herself from developing any further feelings for him. *Although my emotions run pretty deep already.*

She hesitated, feeling vulnerable due to her worries about Sarah. "Can I come over again tomorrow after work though?"

He smiled. "Of course. I was hoping you'd say that." He hugged her tightly.

She held him in return, the sting of tiny tears in her eyes. But she didn't let them surface and brought herself under control before she drew away.

After Eva got home, she dreamed about Damon all night. The recurring theme being her reaching for him and grasping his hand, but him being pulled away by Sarah.

* * * *

The next day when Eva reached Damon's, they managed to make it to the hallway before falling in a heap and having sex on the floor. On Wednesday they made it to the living room sofa, on Thursday they were halfway up the stairs and on Friday they'd gone to the kitchen to fix drinks first, but their plan of taking them to bed fell by the wayside as they succumbed against the kitchen counter.

After they eventually got upstairs with their glasses of wine, they lay in bed talking about their days, sipping at their drinks. Damon's phone started buzzing with Sarah's number. He looked at Eva.

She gestured towards the phone. "Answer it." She took a sip of her drink, trying to pretend she wasn't thrown.

He did as he was told. "Hi. Whoa, slow down... What happened? Back to coronary care? I thought he was doing okay on the general ward?"

Eva's heart sank, but this time not for selfish reasons. She searched Damon's face as he spoke.

He rubbed his forehead. "It's okay. Everything will be alright. I promise."

Eva wanted to reach out and hold his hand but somehow couldn't, like it wasn't hers to hold. After a couple of more minutes, he came off the phone. Eva waited for him to speak, feeling sick.

Damon sighed. "He's had to go back to coronary care. They think he might've had another heart attack. They're running some tests."

Eva shook her head. "I'm so sorry. I don't know what to say. Is he stable?"

"I think so. It's hard to tell," Damon said. "Sarah was too upset to get much sense out of her."

"Do you think you should go over there?" Eva asked.

"No, they only allow two visitors, and Sarah and her mum are there," Damon said. "Our neighbour is watching the kids."

"Are you worried about them?" Eva said. "We could go and get them." She set her wineglass onto the bedside table and made to get out of bed. "I haven't drunk much of my wine, so I can drive us."

Damon looked at her for a second then took her hand, pulling her back towards him. He had that funny expression again, the one she couldn't fathom. It always seemed to occur when they were discussing Sarah.

"It's okay, Evie. But thank you," he said, brushing her hair from her face. "They're asleep already and our neighbour is just in the house until Sarah gets back."

Eva nodded. She couldn't say anything else in case she burst into tears. She hated herself for being so selfish at such a difficult time.

Damon lay back. "Do you want to have another glass of wine and stay over tonight? The kids won't be coming till lunchtime."

Eva struggled with her willpower, wanting to say no because of her natural instinct to protect herself from her feelings because he clearly didn't reciprocate them. But she wanted so desperately to be with him...so she said yes.

Chapter Twenty

Eva was in the shower on Saturday night, trying to wash away her tension. Before she'd left Damon's that morning he'd asked her to stay and go for lunch with him and the kids, but she'd made an excuse to leave because she was becoming more afraid of her emotions.

She'd stayed awake a lot of the night watching Damon sleeping, thinking how handsome he was, how caring, how sexy. Then she remembered the softness in his voice when he was comforting Sarah on the phone.

She was falling for him all over again and she needed to stop herself because he was still in love with Sarah. It wasn't that what she had with him wasn't good. But to him it was obviously just lust, two friends having sex and nothing more. He didn't care for her the way she did for him. *And he never has.* She thought back to their school days and the exact same predicament of being in love with him and him not knowing she was alive. At least now she had a physical relationship with him.

Eva decided that over the weekend she'd stay away and try to collect herself, but it was by no means easy. She thought about him constantly, and her resolve seriously weakened on Sunday night when he messaged to ask her if she'd come over after the kids had gone home. She was about to reply to accept, then she remembered the look in his eyes when they were discussing Sarah. So she made another excuse and said she'd call him on Monday after work.

Everything okay?

Fine, thanks. Just exhausted and need to be on the ball at work tomorrow.

No problem. Speak soon xx

Damon wasn't far from her thoughts at work. She was able to concentrate in the short ten-minute bursts that she was consulting with patients, but in between times when she was completing notes, she really had to focus. For once she didn't mind that there wasn't time to leave her desk for lunch, because she wasn't hungry.

The afternoon clinic passed more slowly and Eva began to grow more nervous about getting home and calling Damon. She didn't know what to do.

Her penultimate patient arrived and her mind zoned in again. As they entered the room, she automatically did her subconscious assessment. She was a young mother carrying a small child. He was one at the most. He appeared lethargic, asleep on his mum's shoulder. His cheeks were flushed.

She smiled at the little boy's mum as she took a seat. "So, what's brought Adam in to see us today?"

"When I collected him from nursery, they said he hadn't been himself this afternoon," Adam's mum said. "He was a bit feverish but not enough for them to call me at work. However, I didn't like the look of him and he felt really hot, so I called to make this appointment."

Eva asked a few more questions: Had he eaten and drank that day? Had he been passing urine normally? Was he unwell the previous day or even that morning? Any cough, vomiting or diarrhoea?

His mum gave all the information, but there wasn't much to go on. He'd been fine when she'd dropped him off, maybe just a snuffly nose and no other symptoms since except the temperature.

Eva asked to examine him, and when his mum turned him around, Eva startled slightly. He looked very similar to another little boy she used to know, one called Oliver. She quashed that thought, focusing on the task at hand.

Adam stirred with the movement and turned his head towards Eva.

"I'm sorry, Doctor," his mum said. "He'll probably kick off now because he never likes being examined."

Eva smiled. "Don't worry. That's no problem."

But Adam didn't cry. He just sat there staring at Eva in a glazed fashion, making her uneasy. She checked him over thoroughly. He did indeed have a fever and a slightly runny nose, so he could have a viral bug on board. His heart rate was a little high and so was his breathing rate. Everything else was normal. He had a slight rash on his body, but it appeared to be a viral rash rather than a sinister one.

Yet Eva was still edgy.

She pointed out the rash to the mum, who said that it hadn't been there when they'd gotten into the car to come to the surgery. Eva explained it was a blanching rash, i.e. it faded with pressure, which meant it didn't fit with a meningitis sort of rash.

Eva verbalized her thoughts. "He has a temperature, and his heart rate and breathing rate are a bit fast," she said. "Now, the latter two things may well be due to the temperature itself. What I'm trying to decide is whether it's just a viral bug giving him the temperature and the other findings, or could there be something else to blame, like a hidden bacterial sort of infection. The rash also looks like it could be due to a virus."

Adam's mum nodded.

"However…" Eva tried to choose her words carefully, "I am a bit worried. You said he had medicine at nursery but his temperature hasn't reduced and he's not behaving normally. You said he'd tend to be upset when examined but he's sitting quite listlessly at the moment." She paused. "I'm not overtly worried, but there's enough for me to say I want you to take him to the paediatric hospital now to be checked out. Would that be okay?"

"Yes of course," Adam's mum said. "I'll go straight away. I was quite worried myself, so I'm happy to take him."

"If you're worried, then that's reason in itself to get checked," Eva said. "I'll do a letter for you to take along."

Eva quickly scribbled a letter for them and handed it over. Adam's mum picked him up and thanked her.

The last patient came in and Eva pushed Adam to the back of her mind while she concentrated. But after they left and she finished her notes and admin for the day he played on her mind more and more. Something wasn't right with him. She remembered her trainer telling her that often in general practice you could feel when something sinister was going on, rather than there being any concrete evidence. Unfortunately, in medicine sinister things didn't always overtly show themselves or present how they logically should.

On the drive home her worry mounted and mounted. Why had he been so listless? Was it just a nasty virus or something more? And the boy's similarity to Oliver started to bother her.

'It will be all right, won't it, Eva? We've caught it in time?'

Eva started to feel panicky. The way she was feeling was down to what had happened in the past rather than the present, but it didn't bring her any comfort.

By the time she got home, she was close to tears. Her parents' car wasn't on the driveway. But in any case, there was only one person she wanted to talk to right now. She reversed back off the drive, heading for Damon's house.

He opened the door with a smile, which morphed into a frown once he took in the look on her face. "What's wrong?"

She came into his arms and he shut the door behind her. Eva stayed silent, her face buried in his shoulder. But she couldn't prevent the tears any longer.

"God, what is it? Are your mum and dad okay?" he asked, his voice rising.

His jumper muffled her speech. "Yes, they're fine. I'm sorry. I'm overreacting about nothing."

He kissed the top of her head. "It doesn't seem like nothing. Come on."

Damon held onto her and led her into the living room, then sat them both onto the sofa. He drew her tightly into him. "Evie, just tell me. Please."

She took a deep breath as he stroked her hair.

Her voice was wobbly. "There was patient today, a one-year-old boy. He became poorly over the day and hopefully it's a virus, but I was worried about him so I got his mum to take him to the hospital to get checked over."

"He's in the right place," Damon said. "You've done the right thing."

"I know, but it mightn't be enough," Eva said, lifting her head to meet his eyes. "That's the trouble in medicine. You can do everything right, everything by the book, but the worst still happens."

Damon paused. "This isn't about the little boy, is it?"

"No. Not this one, anyway," she said.

Damon stayed silent, stroking her cheek.

Eva swallowed. "The place where I worked before was in a small town on the outskirts of the city," she said. "Callum and I lived there, and I also worked at the local surgery. It was quite nice knowing all the patients — but it had its downsides."

"Like people trying to consult you in the supermarket?" Damon asked gently.

Eva gave a tiny laugh. "Yeah, that was one issue." She played with the V-neck of his sweater. "Callum and I had a few friends in the town, but our closest ones were Mel and Andrew. They'd been trying for a baby for ages by the time we first met, and Mel confided in me about it. So I told her to make an appointment for some tests and get referred to the fertility clinic. To be honest, I hadn't meant for her to see me in particular. It's best not to treat friends or family, but she chose to see me and I didn't want to discourage her and hurt her feelings." Eva paused for breath.

Damon watched her, an intense look in his eyes.

"Anyway," Eva continued. "They got referred and waited and waited for IVF treatment. It was so stressful for them, and Mel and I became really close friends over that time. They were one of the lucky couples for which it worked the first time, though the odds were against them. They had baby Oliver, and it was brilliant. We were so happy for them. They asked Callum and I to be his godparents and I was delighted."

Eva had to stop at that point because the tears overflowed again.

Damon hugged her. "Take your time."

She breathed in and out against his chest, his scent soothing her. "It was all good for a while. Then just before Oliver turned one, Mel called to say he appeared pale and was bruising easily. So I said to get him checked out as soon as possible. She did and again made the appointment with me, very soon after we'd spoken. I took one look at him and sent him up to the hospital the same day." She paused. "The next day he was diagnosed with leukaemia."

"Blood cancer?" Damon asked.

"Yes," Eva said quietly.

Damon sighed.

"We acted on it as soon as she noticed the symptoms," Eva said. "And the hospital did everything they could. Mel wanted me to come to all the big appointments with her and Andrew for my medical perspective, so I took annual leave to go with them. But in the end, it was just too aggressive." She shut her eyes. "I remember the day the consultant had to break it to us that it was terminal."

'Eva, what are we going to do? Please don't let it be true...'

Damon hugged her tight. "Evie, I'm so sorry. That's why you were upset about that film."

Eva sighed. "Yeah, it caught me off guard. I should've checked what it was about beforehand."

Damon frowned. "Was all this going on when you caught Callum with Hannah?"

Eva nodded against his chest. "Yes. He knew all about Oliver's diagnosis and treatment, and how much he meant to me as my godson, even though the honour didn't seem to mean much to him. I kept trying to speak to him about it, but he was working late all the time. Well, working on Hannah, anyway." Nausea washed over her as she spoke. "The day I came home and caught them together was the day Oliver died. I was sent home early because I was upset, and I wanted to talk to Callum."

Damon tensed. "That absolute fucking bastard."

She squeezed him tightly. "Don't worry. He got his comeuppance."

Damon relaxed a little. "When you threw them out of the house stark naked?"

"Yeah, well, there's a bit more detail," Eva said, lifting her head. "I lost it. I hardly ever get angry, but after all the stress… Then, when it dawned on me what he'd been doing that whole time with everything poor little Oliver was going through, I saw red. I screamed at them and threw a vase and it smashed right next to their heads. The two of them were terrified. I threw them out, went upstairs and chucked the entire contents of his wardrobe out of the bedroom window. Then finally I threw out Callum's car keys so they could get off my property."

Damon smiled. "Sorry… I know it's not funny, but I think it's karma that he got what he deserved."

Eva shrugged "I don't care about him anymore. The cracks were already starting to show in our relationship way before Oliver got ill. I was pretty fed up with his selfishness. Then after this all happened, I discovered that even though I felt humiliated, I was relieved to be rid of him." She met Damon's gaze. "Oh, the other thing is that after we got the lawyers involved and the house sold, I heard from a mutual friend that there was trouble in paradise."

"How come?" Damon asked, wiping the remnants of Eva's tears from her cheeks.

"The sad little cow obviously thought our nice house and contents were all down to Callum's salary and that I was some sort of desperate housewife," Eva said. "That was probably the picture he deliberately painted. Not that I earn a fortune, but it was at least fifty-fifty in terms of what we brought into the household." She sighed. "After our incomes were no longer joint, he could only afford a much smaller place and she was none too happy. They were rowing a lot and on the rocks, the last I heard."

Damon shook his head. "For God's sake, they deserve each other." He stroked her cheek. "You do know that none of this was your fault, don't you? What happened to Oliver? What happened with Callum?"

"Yeah, I know." Eva hugged him again. "But it doesn't make it any better. It was after all that that I decided to leave the practice and come home. And no way was I going to work in the same town I lived in again. I also promised myself not to get too emotionally involved with any more patients — and look at me now."

Damon kissed the top of her head. "What happened to Mel and Andrew?"

Eva sighed. "They were devastated, obviously. Yet Mel was still so lovely and supportive to me when she eventually heard what had happened with Callum. I felt so guilty that she was giving me any sympathy after what she'd been through."

"Have you spoken to her since you moved?" Damon asked.

Eva shook her head. "Not yet, I haven't been able to bring myself to." She paused. "I know it's selfish."

"It's not selfish," Damon said. "You're just trying to heal. But I do think it'd be helpful to the both of you if you contacted her."

"I know. You're right," Eva said.

Damon hesitated. "Why don't you call the hospital to check on the little boy? It might help you to know what's happening."

Eva thought about it. She shouldn't get too involved, but she really needed to know if he was okay. "Yes, I think I will. Thank you."

She lifted out her mobile and called the hospital. She explained to the nurse at the other end who she was and why she was calling. The nurse went to check what was happening and gain permission from Adam's mum to update her.

When Eva hung up, fresh tears welled in her eyes. "He's deteriorated. They think it actually *is* meningitis and he's getting treated for it."

Damon rubbed his forehead. "Shit. I thought you were going to say it was all fine."

"See what I mean?" Eva said. "Sometimes these things don't show themselves and that's when you can get caught out."

"I know, sweetheart. But you *did* catch it, and you've done everything you can." Damon drew her back into him. "Do you want to stay here tonight? Just to sleep, I mean," he added quickly. "Then in the morning you can call again to see how he is before you go to work."

Eva considered it, remembering her previous vow to keep Damon at arm's length emotionally. But her resolve collapsed. "Yes, thanks, I'd really like that."

Damon made them both something to eat, and after that, Eva was dead on her feet so they went upstairs to bed. Damon gave her a T-shirt and some shorts to wear as pyjamas.

Eva got changed while Damon stripped to his underwear, and after she was finished, she caught him watching her.

"Not the sexiest bed wear, is it?" she quipped.

"It is on you," he said softly.

Eva borrowed a spare toothbrush then the two of them climbed into bed. She was exhausted to her core, yet somehow lighter for having shared things with Damon. It didn't take long for her to drop off, but the feeling of unease lingered again as she realised she'd tethered herself even more tightly to him emotionally. She clung to him as she drifted off, her final conscious thought going round her head.

I'm in serious trouble here.

Chapter Twenty-One

In the morning Eva called the hospital again but was told there would be no more news until the ward round had been completed.

Eva hugged Damon goodbye and promised to let him know when she heard about Adam. He had that strange look in his eyes again. Had he spoken to Sarah while she was in the bathroom?

She headed home to shower and change into fresh clothes for work. Then she made her way back into the surgery. She decided to call the hospital straight after morning clinic was done. The ward round should be finished by then. As she went from patient to patient, Adam wasn't far from her thoughts and neither was Damon. Finally, the last person left her room and she lifted the phone to call the hospital. She waited patiently for them to answer, then again while the nurse went to check the information.

"There's good news this morning, Dr. Mathers," the nurse said when she came back to the phone. "Adam's stabilized well overnight with the antibiotics, and the consultant is pleased with his progress. Hopefully, he'll be moved out of the special care unit soon."

Eva sighed. "That's brilliant news. Thank you so much for finding out for me." Relief flooded through her like a warm, soothing liquid. She called Damon.

"Evie?"

"I just got off the phone with the hospital. It's fine. He's doing a lot better."

He sighed. "Thank goodness. There's more good news too. Sarah's dad is doing well. He didn't have another heart attack after all and he's back on the normal ward."

Eva smiled. "Brilliant. It's about time we had positive news."

"Definitely," Damon said. "I reckon our fortunes are changing. Sarah wants me to go out for a family dinner tomorrow night with her and the kids, but can I see you tonight? We can go out if you like."

A family dinner? What if the situation with her dad had made Sarah realise what she'd thrown away with Damon and she wanted to ask him back? Eva should probably stay away and take up camp behind her emotional wall again. But then again, if Damon and Sarah were going to end up back together and Eva's heart was inevitably broken, surely she should make the most of her time with Damon before it all came crashing down around her ears.

"Yes, let's meet tonight," she said. "But I don't want to go out. I'll come over to yours. I'd like you to myself."

"You got it," Damon said. "I'll see you soon."

Eva finished the day feeling much lighter than the previous evening. She drove over to Damon's. He was smiling as he opened the door to greet her and she went straight into his arms.

"Come on," she said, taking his hand. "This time we're finally going to make it to the bedroom."

She led him up the stairs and into the room. Damon tugged her hand gently and brought her into him to kiss her. Smiling against her mouth, he collapsed them both onto the bed.

Eva tried to drink in everything about him—his warm brown eyes and the way his hair fell onto his forehead, the scent of his skin and the soft, exquisite friction of it against hers, the feel of his lips moving over her mouth, then the fiery tide of sensation they elicited as he grazed them down her body to reach her most intimate areas.

He licked and teased her until she nearly lost control but stopped short of taking her over the edge, so in tune with her body that he knew exactly how close he could get her.

He raised himself up to rest his forehead against hers as he gradually inched inside her. Everything he did was slow and considered. Each movement intensified the already unbearable ache in her pelvis and the look in his eyes was so intense that it was as if she was drowning in them.

Eva discovered that she hadn't experienced something this powerful before—and not just in the physical sense. That was her last coherent thought before she lost herself in rapture.

Damon kissed her as he thrust deeper. He moaned her name against her lips, the sound of it intensifying her pleasure impossibly further until its swell overwhelmed her. It lifted inside her, the breath leaving her body as it reached a crescendo on a fierce tide of emotion.

Damon collapsed onto her, holding her tightly, the sound of his breathing laboured at her ear.

She wrapped her arms around him, the last remnants of her emotional wall tumbling down. That was it. There was no denying she'd fallen for him.

She buried her face in his neck and breathed him in, savouring the delicious feeling of his body against hers, their skin in the ultimate head-to-toe contact.

Eva didn't know how long they lay there holding each other until Damon rolled to her side and drew her into his body. They both drifted off to sleep.

In the morning Eva awoke first, seeing Damon and happily remembering where she was. She stroked his cheek. He was so beautiful when he was sleeping.

Damon opened his eyes and a slow smile spread across his face. He reached out and pulled her towards him. "Mmm." He kissed her neck. "It wasn't just a fantastic dream then. Last night was amazing."

She smiled. "You can pat yourself on the back. I can't remember it ever being that good before."

He brushed her hair behind her ear. "You mean not with Callum?"

"I mean not with anyone," Eva said. "Not that I've got a lot of notches on my bedpost. You're only the third."

He grinned. "I'm still taking that as a compliment."

She laughed. "You should, because it is."

He bent his elbow under his head. "I'm only a couple of notches up from you, so let's call it even. Hey, you know who my first was, but who was yours?"

"Brian," she said.

"That guy you went out with at college?"

"Yep, that's right." Eva grinned. "Unfortunately, he didn't have the experience of Tracey McKenna, but he did his best."

Damon groaned and rubbed his temples with his fingers. "Don't even mention her name."

Eva manoeuvred herself so that her back was pushed against Damon's chest. "Come on," she said. "You must've liked her at the time."

He played with her hair. "She dragged me into a bush and stripped us both naked," he said. "I was sixteen years old and all us lads were bothered about at the time was losing the V-plates. We didn't really care who with."

"Ugh," Eva said. "That's so unromantic." She nestled her back further into him, enjoying the sensation of his hands in her hair. "You know," she said, "I think we should give Tracey a break. Martina told Jane that Tracey really did like you, even back when we were sixteen. She wanted you to ask her out, and seducing you in a bush was her way of letting you know that. But even though it wasn't a very subtle tactic, you still didn't ask her, and that was all that ever happened between you. She must've felt pretty used, as well as disappointed."

Even though she and Tracey had opposite approaches, Tracey stripping both herself and Damon naked versus Eva refusing to speak to him at all, they both were infatuated with him and so Eva could understand and empathise with Tracey's feelings.

Damon sighed. "You're making me feel really bad now. I just thought I was the latest in her line of conquests. She never gave me any reason to think otherwise, and I wouldn't ever have made the first move with her. All joking aside, she really wasn't my type." He paused. "I should've had the sense to throw her off back then as well."

Eva shook her head. "Don't feel bad. That's not what I'm getting at. You were only a teenager and you're right that hormones ruled our heads at that age. The main thing is that you wouldn't make the same mistake now, whereas the likes of Callum are still so driven by testosterone that they can't keep it in their pants, despite being grown men."

Damon kissed her ear. "I'm not surprised you're sympathising with Tracey — and with the teenage me. You're always so understanding of everyone else's point of view."

She laughed. "Yeah, just not Callum's."

"No," Damon said, nuzzling into her hair. "He'll always remain a douchebag in my book."

Eva turned her head towards him, smiling. "Are you sniffing my hair?"

He nestled his face further into her curls. "Yeah, totally. I'm not ashamed to admit I'm addicted to your scent. You smell like summertime."

Eva laughed and turned her head back again. "What about the other girlfriends pre-Sarah? I assume you liked them."

"Yeah, but I didn't love them. Sarah was the first one I loved," Damon said.

Eva attempted to drown out the voice in her head, the one telling her that Sarah was still the one he loved. She tried to stifle it by talking. "That's interesting," she said. "I can't imagine what that's like. I've been in love with everyone I've slept with."

Even before she uttered the last syllable, she understood the implication of what she'd said and wished she could grab the words from the air and stuff them back in her mouth. Thank goodness she was facing away from him so that he couldn't see her face. Would he put two and two together? *Of course he will.*

His voice was quiet. "Eva —"

"Shit! Look at the time. I've got an early clinic today." Eva jumped out of the bed and scooped her clothes, sweeping everything into the bathroom. She quickly washed and dressed, then burst out of the bathroom past where Damon was sitting in bed with a confused expression on his face.

She ran to the front door, calling up the stairs as she went. "Sorry, Damon! I hope your dinner tonight goes well. I'll phone you."

She thought she heard him call her name down the stairs just before she slammed the door and roared off in her car.

At lunchtime Eva's phone rang with Damon's number and she ignored it. A voicemail flashed but she didn't listen. She was too scared of what it might say.

By the time she got home that evening, she'd had another two missed calls from him and two more voicemails. There was no way she was going to pick them up. She imagined Damon letting her down gently, telling her that he didn't see what they had going anywhere beyond friends with benefits.

Eva called Rachel and told her everything about Adam and how she'd confided in Damon, plus more detail regarding Oliver than she'd ever disclosed previously. It was as if letting Damon in had enabled her to do the same with her other loved ones.

Rachel listened quietly.

By the time Eva got to the part about how she had fallen for Damon and accidentally given it away, she was in tears.

"Don't cry, Evie," Rachel said. "It's not that bad."

"How could it be any worse?" Eva said. "He's out with Sarah right now and she's probably telling him she wants him back. He'll be ecstatic because he still loves her and so excited to have his family together again. He really misses living with the kids, you know."

"I don't doubt that," Rachel said. "However, I seriously doubt that he still loves Sarah."

"How do you know?" Eva asked.

"I just do. If you really want my opinion, I think he loves *you*," Rachel said.

Eva shook her head. "I don't think so."

"Come on," Rachel said. "You've made leaps and bounds with all this emotional stuff and I think it's brilliant. But you just need to go that extra mile. You have to tell him how you really feel. You can't be scared."

"Yes, I can," Eva said.

"Eva. This isn't going to go away if you ignore it. Be honest with Damon."

Eva sighed. "I'll just bury it and eventually I'll get over him...like I got over Callum."

"That was different," Rachel said. "And it's totally messed you up for future relationships. You're too scared to let yourself be vulnerable because you were hurt so badly last time. You can't let that be Callum's legacy."

Eva hesitated. "I don't know."

"Just promise me you'll think about it," Rachel said.

Eva's head swam as she tried to process everything. "I'll try."

"I'm going to call you tomorrow to see what you've decided," Rachel said. "I'm not going to let up until you take action."

"Careful, Rach, or I'll start ditching your calls," Eva said.

"Okay, okay. I'm still calling you, though."

After Eva ended hung up, she lay on her bed and stared at the ceiling, her mind on Damon. Funny, she could remember being in this exact same position thinking about him when she was at school. Life hadn't moved on at all. She sighed and tried to stop imagining him kissing Sarah at the end of the evening. Eventually, once her mind had exhausted itself, she fell asleep.

She awoke with a start a couple of hours later. Her phone was buzzing on the bedside table. Damon was calling again. She stared at the phone, trying to summon the willpower to answer. She thought about what Rachel had said. She was right that Callum had messed everything up for her with his gaslighting. She shouldn't let him get away with affecting her current emotional choices but she just couldn't bring herself to pick up the phone.

Eva lay back on the bed and stared at the ceiling as the phone rang off and beeped with yet another voicemail. She stared into the darkness.

Chapter Twenty-Two

The next working day passed in a cloud of misery for Eva. A few times she lifted her phone, intending to at least listen to the voicemails, but she chickened out at the last minute every time. On one occasion she nearly dialled Damon's number, but after she hovered her finger over the call button for a few seconds, she put the phone back down. It was probably for the best if she just didn't speak to him for a while, let him get on with things with Sarah and make a clean break.

She arrived home from work dejected. She was miserable without Damon and it'd only been thirty-six hours since she'd seen him. In her mind's eye, a lifetime without him stretched before her.

She entered the house and practically tripped over a suitcase. "What the?"

"Eva? Is that you?" Meena called from the kitchen.

"Yeah. What's this case doing here?" Eva called back.

Her mum appeared in the hallway. "It's our long weekend away. Remember?"

Eva had forgotten that her parents were going away that evening until Sunday night. *Great. Three whole nights alone, pining for Damon*. The situation was getting more depressing by the minute.

"Yeah, that's right," Eva said. "Are you all set?"

Meena nodded. "The taxi's coming."

"Right now?" Eva said.

"Yes"." Meena looked at Eva. "*Beti*, do you want us to cancel?"

"No," Eva said. "Of course not. Why would I want that?"

Meena frowned. "We can tell something has happened. You didn't eat a thing last night and I heard you crying on the phone when I passed your bedroom door." She touched Eva's arm. "Is it Damon?" she asked softly.

Eva hesitated, then nodded.

Meena led her into the kitchen and within a couple of minutes the inevitable cup of tea was set in front of her

Eva sighed. "I'm not sure what to do."

Meena appeared unruffled. "Tell him that you're in love with him."

Eva raised her eyebrows. "How do you know I'm in love with him?"

Meena smiled. "I've always known how you felt about him. I'm your mother. I can tell these things. Why do you think I've been trying to interfere?"

Eva rubbed her forehead. "He doesn't feel the same way."

"Of course he does. Lily told me."

Eva snapped her head up. "He told Auntie Lily that?"

Meena shook her head. "No, but she can tell too. It's the motherly instinct."

Eva laughed, despite the sadness gripping her heart. "I think he *is* in love with someone, but it's not me."

Just then a car horn sounded from the front of the house.

"There's the taxi," Meena said. "Are you sure we shouldn't cancel? It's no problem if you need us."

"No," Eva said. "You've been looking forward to it and you and Dad deserve the time together. I'll be fine, honestly."

Matthew went out of the front door to take their luggage to the taxi.

Meena stood and kissed Eva's cheek. "Just talk to him. Anything is better than the agony of not knowing. You really aren't protecting yourself from anything."

Eva couldn't reply. The lump in her throat was too big. She stood and hugged her mum goodbye, then followed her to the front door and waved her off as she left the house to climb into the taxi. Her dad was speaking to the taxi driver.

Matthew came back to the door after depositing the bags. "Bye, we'll bring you something back from Paris," he said, kissing Eva on the cheek.

"Thanks. Have fun," Eva said

Matthew turned back as he went through the door. "Damon's a good lad, you know."

Eva smiled. She shouldn't be surprised that he knew what was going on. He always quietly read every situation. Ever since reunion night, she'd had a feeling that her dad had deliberately taken his time in getting to the front door that evening, as if he'd known that Damon was outside with her.

He closed the door gently behind him, and Eva went up the stairs. She busied herself about her room, changing her work clothes for some yoga pants and a vest top. She had a notion that she might do an online class after dinner to try to unwind.

As she pulled on the vest, she was aware of footsteps on the stairs and her bedroom door opening.

She turned. "What did you forget, Mum?"

Damon stood in the doorway looking as hot as hell. Eva sucked in her breath.

He leaned against the door. "Your mum and dad have gone. I arrived as they were getting into the taxi and your dad let me in. I hope you don't mind."

Eva shook her head, shocked into silence. He was wearing a smart pair of fitted grey work trousers and a black shirt. He looked gorgeous.

His voice was gentle. "You've been dodging my calls." He moved towards her. "What's going on?"

Her feet were rooted to the spot. She stared at the floor. "Nothing."

Why is he still moving closer? Why does he look so good? Good God, why does he smell so good?

Damon stood in front of her. He touched her bare shoulder and gently dragged his fingers along her arm, causing goosebumps to erupt in his wake. He took her hand and her breath caught in her throat.

"Eva, look at me."

She lifted her gaze from where she'd been studying the carpet and immediately lost herself in his eyes.

"You need to talk to me," Damon said softly. "What's going on with you? I had the best night of my life then in the morning you disappeared, and you've been ducking my calls since." He tucked her hair behind her ear. "I think I might know why, but I want to hear it from you."

Eva's heart went into overdrive. She couldn't say it. She hadn't spoken those words since the days she was pleading with Callum to come home and support her, to no avail. What if she was let down again?

She swallowed hard and opened her mouth, but it was so dry that she couldn't form any words at all.

Damon took hold of her shoulder gently. He gazed into her eyes and she was sure he was reading her soul. "You don't have to be scared with me. I'm not Callum. He emotionally abused you and that's not me. There's no way I would ever hurt you. Just tell me how you feel."

Eva managed to find her voice. "I can't."

"Why not? You can tell me anything," he said. "I thought we'd got past the wall that you've built around yourself."

She took a deep breath. "I can't, because you don't feel the same way I do."

Damon frowned. "There's no way you believe that. You can't possibly think this was just about sex to me?"

Eva stared at him, thrown. "I...I don't know."

Damon sighed. "Evie." He ran his fingers through her hair. "Okay, fine. If you can't say it, then I will." He held her head gently, keeping her gaze on him as a whooshing noise sounded in her ears. "I am so in love with you. I can't stop thinking about you and it's driving me crazy." He brushed his thumb across her cheek. "I love how caring you are and the way you tune into everyone else's feelings, especially mine. I love how great you are with Adele and Sam. You're my best friend and I've never been as attracted to someone in my whole life."

Eva's heart soared so high at those words that she felt lightheaded. Her pulse raced as she gazed at him, not wanting him to stop speaking.

His trailed his thumb across her lower lip. "You're the sexist woman alive, and all I want to do is make love to you all day every day—because that's what we've been doing, not just having sex. That fact can't have escaped you. And you must've seen it on my face over the past couple of weeks too, because I haven't been able to hide it."

She remembered that funny look in his eye. "What about Sarah?"

He frowned. "What's she got to do with anything?"

Eva hesitated. Had she got it all wrong? "I thought you were still in love with her. You were so lovely and supportive when her dad was ill. I thought it'd stirred old feelings and that she'd want you back too."

Damon shook his head. "I haven't loved Sarah that way in a very long time—and she feels exactly the same. We care about each other because we have kids together but that's it."

"She didn't want you to go to dinner to ask you to get back together?" Eva said.

Damon frowned. "Of course not."

Eva rubbed her forehead. "I'm so sorry. I misread everything."

He took her hands in his. "To be honest, I'm not surprised. After everything with Callum, I think it has left you traumatized. You couldn't open up to anyone because you were scared of being hurt again. I do understand." He paused. "But I need to reiterate that I'm not him. I love you, I'm here for you and you can trust me. I will never, ever let you down."

He leaned in to kiss her, and she melted into him. He murmured against her lips. "Tell me, Evie. I need to hear you say it."

She wrapped her arms around his neck, studying him intently as her love for him overwhelmed her. His words had given her the courage to speak from the heart. "I love you so much, more than I've ever loved anyone." She stroked her fingers along his cheek. "To be honest, I think I always have."

He sighed and smiled, resting his forehead against hers, then he kissed her again. "I can't tell you how good it feels to hear you say that," he said. "I suspected you felt the same when you said you'd never slept with someone you weren't in love with, but I have to admit I panicked when you bolted."

Eva screwed her face up at the thought of him being hurt by her actions. "I'm sorry for being such an idiot."

He rubbed his nose against hers. "I'm pretty sure I could forgive you anything."

She brought her head up to meet his and kissed him. It didn't take long for heat to start building within her and she backed them towards the bed.

Damon drew away. "Hold on. I need to say something before we go any further."

Eva's heart sank. "What is it?"

He met her gaze. "This is it now, no more holding back—no more secrets and no more walls. I want you to tell me everything and trust that I'll be there to support you." He placed his hand over her heart. "I want it all, Evie. I want all of you."

Eva nodded, a delicious warmth seeping through her body. "I promise."

He leaned in to kiss her again but she stopped him, planting her hand on his chest. "On that note, I have one more thing to say."

He raised his eyebrow. "Oh yeah?"

Eva spoke quickly before she could change her mind. "I had a massive crush on you at school. I used to daydream about you and stare at you in class, wishing you'd ask me out."

Damon's mouth fell open. "What?"

"Yeah…" Eva said. It was more embarrassing than she'd thought. She took a deep breath, aware that her face was flushing. "I used to lie in this bed at night and imagine that you might be my first."

He frowned. "I thought you hated me at school?"

"No way," Eva said. "Why would you think that?"

Damon shook his head. "You didn't even want to talk to me. If I spoke to you, you'd tell me to get lost and flounce off."

"I did that because I fancied you," Eva said. "I ran away because I was embarrassed, and I didn't know what to say. Plus, I thought you were out of my league."

"Out of your league?" Damon said. "I thought *you* were out of *mine*. You were so clever I thought you'd figured you were above me."

Eva shook her head so hard that it hurt her neck. "I would never think that."

Damon laughed. "Bloody hell. We really should've talked more." He paused. "But what about before you got together with Brian, when I saw you out in town and I came over to congratulate you on your exam results?"

Eva frowned. "What about it?"

"I was making a move on you, Eva."

"What?" She raised her eyebrows. That couldn't be true. "I thought you were just being nice."

"I *was* being nice" — Damon grinned — "in order to make a move."

She laughed. "I can't believe I missed that. I would've been so up for it, too."

Damon looked at her, still smiling. "There was another time as well."

Eva's mouth fell open. "You've got to be kidding me."

"Nope," he said. "After you split with Brian and before you got together with Callum, you were home from university for the weekend, and I offered to buy you a twenty-first birthday drink at the Swan."

Eva remembered it. "I thought you were consoling me after Brian and I broke up, and someone else was already getting me a drink, so I said no thanks and gave you a hug."

Damon grinned. "Again, I *was* trying to console you…but also making a move."

Eva shook her head "You would've been better off clubbing me over the head. I'm so dense."

Damon laughed. "Don't worry. I still love you."

Eva smiled. She loved hearing him say that. "I'm sorry you struck out. Come here and let me make it up to you." She grasped his shirt to pull him into a kiss, then started unbuttoning the shirt.

"Now that you mention it," he said against her mouth. "My feelings *were* rather hurt…"

He backed her onto the bed then lay over her and looked into her eyes, stealing kisses from her lips as he spoke. "I may have missed out on being your first," he whispered. "But I have to tell you I fully intend to be your last."

Then he slowly and tenderly made love to her, on the bed where she'd spent so many hours dreaming of him.

Epilogue

Damon opened the door of the beach house and put his sunglasses on as sunlight reflected off the white sand and dazzled his eyes. He walked out from the air-conditioned room onto the veranda, the heat blasting his skin, and surveyed the private stretch of beach that was theirs for their honeymoon.

The small island in the Maldives was beautiful, and in a couple of days when they jetted off, they wouldn't be returning home to Oakcastle but to meet Sarah, her partner Stewart and Adele and Sam for a family holiday in Sri Lanka. Then once they were eventually home, it wouldn't be long before they'd be travelling to Edinburgh for a long weekend with Mel and Andrew.

Back when Eva had first called Mel from Yorkshire to have a heart to heart, it was gratefully received. They'd talked frequently on the phone over the proceeding weeks and months, and Mel and Andrew had been pleased to accept Eva and Damon's wedding invitation when the time came. At the wedding, the

Scottish couple had privately disclosed the fantastic news that they were expecting another baby, this time naturally. It was a miracle that they'd never dreamed of in the aftermath of their loss. The look of utter joy on Eva's face when she'd heard the news was by far the best wedding present Damon could ever have gotten.

Damon scanned the water's edge. Where was his lovely wife? His heart beat faster when he laid eyes on her. She never failed to quicken his pulse. He admired her tanned body as she stood with her back to him in her black bikini. He drifted his eyes up her shapely legs, along the curve of her bottom and hips and over the swell of her breasts in her bikini top as she angled her torso sideways, her hand on her forehead shielding her eyes as she looked out over the sea. He stood silently, watching her. She turned farther towards him, finally spotting his presence.

She smiled and started walking over the sand in his direction. *She's so beautiful.* His heart pounded. It was the end of their second week in the Maldives and they'd been having sex at least three times a day, yet he still couldn't get enough of her. There wasn't an inch of her body that he hadn't yet explored, but the sight of her still drove him crazy. Lust stirred deep inside him as she approached. They'd already made love that morning, but he was more than ready for her again.

She reached the wooden stairs of the veranda and climbed into his arms. He lifted his sunglasses onto the top of his head as she took hers off.

Eva put her arms around his neck and he savoured her beautiful body pressing against his. She smiled and kissed him. "Afternoon, sleepyhead. I thought you were never going to wake up. I've been waiting for you."

She ran her hand down his bare chest onto the front of his swim shorts. His breathing picked up. He smiled as he gazed into her gorgeous green eyes.

"I was just recharging myself for you," he said.

Eva smiled and slipped her hand inside the shorts. He drew in breath against her mouth as she kissed him slowly. They came up for air and he rested his forehead against hers. She removed her hand and gestured towards the beach house. Damon gave her smile, then scooped her into his arms to carry her through the patio doors and onto the emperor-sized bed.

He studied her for a moment, propped on her elbows, her tanned skin and dark bikini contrasting against the white sheets.

"Now that is one view I will never, ever tire of," he said.

Damon crawled over her slowly, before stripping off the small amount of material they were both wearing and making love to her for the second, but unlikely the last, time that day.

Want to see more from this author? Here's a taster for you to enjoy!

Revealed
Zoe Allison

Excerpt

A loud crack pierced the moonlit darkness of the trees. Amber peered out from the large fir she was crouching behind. She couldn't see Victoria through the cover of darkness, but she could sense exactly where she was. Amber lifted her hand and gestured toward the noise, indicating for Victoria to proceed with the plan.

Amber closed her eyes. She felt Victoria's presence move away, closer to the target. Louder and louder noises emanated through the wilderness from that same direction. The target was clearly distracted by his human prey and unaware that they were closing in on him. Amber took the opportunity to stealthily rise and creep closer herself. She could sense that he would soon be in her line of vision.

Then there he was, in a small clearing among the firs. He crouched over the limp form of his victim, snarling as he took his fill of blood. Amber darted her gaze over the clearing to where Victoria was hiding in the darkness. Their eyes met, and Amber nodded almost imperceptibly.

Victoria leaped toward the man. As she flew through the air she snarled, revealing her extended razor-sharp canine teeth. He snapped up his head from his distraction, blood smearing his face and dripping from his own pointed eyeteeth. However, his reaction had come too late. Victoria slammed into him, knocking him off the body and rolling him farther into the clearing. She pinned him to the ground and slammed her fist so hard into his face that the impact drove his head into the earth below. He was strong from his feed, however, and his sharp reflexes kicked in. He flung the bottom half of his body upward in a forceful jab, sending Victoria over the top of his head, where she tumbled over the forest floor and landed lightly on her feet. She circled him as he rose to standing and the two of them faced off a few yards apart.

Victoria smiled, tossing her long blonde hair over her shoulder. She lifted her hand, turned her palm upward and brought her fingers toward herself in an invitation to the fight. Her insolent gesture had the desired effect. He growled, and in a blind rage ran in her direction. She had already pulled back her arm and, as he reached her, she smashed her fist into his face, sending him hurtling away toward the tree line, where he crashed into a thick trunk, cracking it in the process. Within a split second Victoria was upon him, pinning him in place. She glanced over at Amber, who was still hidden a few feet away, and nodded.

Amber was by Victoria's side quickly, even though, unlike her partner, she wasn't capable of vampire speed. The man's black, dead-looking eyes met hers, and registered her human form. A sneer appeared on his face as he started to thrash in an attempt to escape Victoria's grip and get at Amber. Before he could gain any purchase, Amber closed in, grabbing hold of the man's head. He screamed in agony, and Victoria stepped away while Amber did her work.

A few seconds later, silence fell. Moonlight shone on the fir-lined clearing, devoid of any presence except a mound of ash sitting beside a cracked tree trunk.

* * * *

Amber leaned against the doorframe of Victoria's bedroom, watching her partner pack her suitcase.

Victoria gestured toward her. "Pass me that wash bag, will you?"

Amber tossed it over, and Victoria caught it deftly in one hand before depositing it on top of the clothes in the suitcase.

Amber lifted her hands and started scraping her jet-black hair into a ponytail. "Got everything?"

Victoria stood back, surveying the room with her hands on her hips. "Yeah, I reckon so." She glanced toward Amber. "Going on your run?"

Amber nodded before grabbing the doorframe with one hand to steady herself while she lifted her leg in a quads stretch. "I'm going to try to beat my personal best for twenty-six miles."

Victoria zipped her bag. "Aiming for two hours then?"

Amber lifted her other leg. "Yep."

Victoria smiled. "A snail's pace."

Amber laughed. "Yeah... Well, it's fast for a human."

Victoria went to the bedroom window and took in the view over the parks and the river from their elevated vantage point at the edge of downtown. "See ya, Calgary. It's been a blast."

She turned back toward Amber. "So, I'll be gone when you get back."

Amber nodded. "Where to now? Back to Australia?"

"Nope." Victoria shook her head. "South America. What about you? Heard anything yet?"

"No," Amber said. "I think they'll call later today after I've finished my training. I'm going to the gym this afternoon then I've got a combat class, so I guess it'll be evening before I hear."

"Cool," Victoria said. "Hope it's somewhere awesome."

Amber smiled at her. "Okay. Well… Have a safe trip." She came toward Victoria and held out her hand.

Victoria took her hand in a shake. "Great working with you. Hopefully we'll be paired again sometime."

Amber let go of Victoria and turned to go. "Yeah, maybe. We'll see what the boss says." She gave a little wave as she left the room, heading for the front door where she would ride the elevator down to the apartment-block exit.

The cold air bit into her skin as she left the building, but she barely registered it. A brisk walk took her to the beginning of the periphery of green around downtown, and there she broke out into her run.

She moved her limbs effortlessly throughout her journey. The air temperature started to rise as the sun shone brightly in the sky. Beams of sunlight glinted off the surface of the river and reflected from the high rises, warming her skin.

Amber completed her two-hour run then dropped her pace slightly to jog back home for a shower. She barely registered the lack of Victoria's presence in the apartment. Their bond had been professional and efficient. Each would have given their life for the other, but yet there wasn't any real emotional attachment between them. They had been trained to not get involved in that way or else a mission could be compromised. In any case, personal ties didn't suit Amber.

After the run, her schedule consisted of a meditation period and an organic lunch. She then went to a martial arts session in the afternoon. She had a training room rented at the local gym, where she practiced set moves for two hours, covering a mixture of karate katas, kickboxing, tai chi and also some gymnastics for good measure. Then she attended a combat class so that she could keep on top of her sparring. She pretty much had to hold back the whole time, so as not to draw attention to herself or land anyone in the hospital. Currently she was on downtime, so she didn't need anything more challenging than that. The schedule's purpose was purely to keep her active until she got the next call.

Once back at the apartment, just as Amber was finishing her evening yoga routine, her phone rang. She knew it would be her new partner, because everyone would know not to call until her training schedule was finished for the day.

She picked up the phone, feeling some anticipation at who it might be. "Hello?"

A familiar male voice answered, one she had not heard in a long time — and the only voice which could elicit an emotional response of any kind in Amber.

"Good evening, Amber Ridley." His voice was flawlessly neutral, giving little clue as to his origins. "You are speaking with your new partner."

Amber registered the unfamiliar sensation of her heart warming. Normally she maintained a very neutral and cool interior, as well as exterior. It wasn't a romantic sort of warming, however, but the sort that came when speaking to a sibling after a long time apart, because Valentino was like a brother to her.

"It's good to hear your voice," she said. "How are you?"

"Oh, you know me, sorella. I am always good."

Amber smiled at the sound of his pet name for her. It meant 'sister' in Italian and he had called her that for as long as she could remember. "So, where am I coming to meet you?" she asked.

"You will leave first thing in the morning for the UK."

"The UK? I haven't been back there since —"

"Since I found you. I know," Vale replied. "But it is not London. It is Scotland this time. I do not think you have been there before."

"No, I haven't," Amber said. "Whereabouts?"

"The mission itself is in Edinburgh, but we shall reside out of the city, in a more uninhabited area. Mr. X wishes us to stay incognito when we are not directly engaged in tracking or combat."

"Okay. I'll meet you at the airport when I land."

"It has been too long, sorella, I am looking forward to us being together again. I will give you more details once we are in Edinburgh."

After the call ended, Amber immediately packed her belongings, and it didn't take long. When one led a frugal life with no intimate or emotional contacts, possessions didn't really accumulate.

Home of Erotic Romance

Sign up for our newsletter and find out about all our romance book releases, eBook sales and promotions, sneak peeks and FREE romance books!

About the Author

Zoe lives in Edinburgh, Scotland with her husband and two children. A medic by day, she started writing in her spare time as a means to counter burn out and found that this was a balm for the soul.

She is a fan of the romantic genre and it's 'happily ever after' ethos. A sharp contrast to what she can, at times, see in her day job. Zoe is keen for the female lead in romantic fiction to disabuse stereotypes and walk on an equal footing with her male counterparts. She prefers male leads who do not display signs of toxic masculinity and believes and that positive masculinity is much more attractive to women and healthier for men.

Zoe loves to hear from readers. You can find her contact information, website details and author profile page at https://www.totallybound.com

Printed in Great Britain
by Amazon

60945801R00128